The Proto Project
A Sci-Fi Adventure of the Mind
By Bryan R. Johnson

When Jason meets his mom's billion-dollar invention, an artificial intelligence device named Proto, he accidentally gets caught up in a mysterious adventure. Proto goes missing, and then people go missing. Now Jason and his coolest-neighbor-ever Maya must risk their lives to prevent global mayhem. But who is behind this devious plot? Is it another AI? The FBI? Or any other abbreviation with an I? What exactly is there to learn about artificial and human intelligence while fighting for your life against a legion of furry puppies or a battalion of drones? A lot— if you live to tell about it.

"The plot is zany and unpredictable, and Johnson's characters are a hoot to watch as they expand their imaginations, skills, and world-views in response to the crisis they're facing. I found this book impossible to put down." ★★★★★
- Jack Magnus, Readers' Favorite

"... A quick-turning, thrilling ride ... Upper elementary readers looking for a fast adventure with a sci-fi setting will likely enjoy Proto and his adventure." RECOMMENDED.
- Mark Heisey, US Reviews

About the Author

Bryan R. Johnson is a real-life adventurer. When he's not climbing the peaks of Mount Kilimanjaro or flying airplanes, he's exploring the inner-workings of the human brain and investing in breakthrough science. Bryan prefers fist bumps over handshakes, hip hop to jazz, and pizza without crust.

More Books by Bryan R. Johnson

Code 7

Cracking the Code for an Epic Life
A funny and fast-paced chapter book, ages 7-10

Mom's Choice Gold Award Winner
Wishing Shelf Book Gold Award Winner
Royal Dragonfly Award Winner

"This book is an inspiration to children who wish to pursue their passions and bring original ideas into the world."

- Adam Grant
New York Times bestselling author

Código 7

Descifrando el código para una vida épica
A bilingual Spanish-English edition of Code 7, ages 7-10

Readers' Favorite Five Star Award ★★★★★

"The stories are awesome, and the opportunity to use both languages while enjoying them is a big plus. Código 7 is most highly recommended."

- Jack Magnus
Readers' Favorite

THE PROTO PROJECT

A Sci-Fi Adventure of the Mind

BRYAN R. JOHNSON

To my children
Genevieve, Talmage, and Jefferson

I hope that the magic of stories remains with you throughout your life; thank you for being wonderful listeners and participants. I love you.

CONTENTS

YOU'VE NEVER SEEN ANYTHING LIKE IT

There were good field trips and bad field trips. The one that Jason was about to embark upon would trigger a series of events that would turn anyone into a whimpering, babbling scaredy-pants, never to board a filthy school bus again. But we can't get into the details about that unless we start from the beginning.

Jason Albert Pascal stared at his reflection in the bath-room mirror while listening to his favorite rock band *Lightning Strikes*. He styled his hair into a perfect mess using a touch of gel, then frowned at the hint of a pimple on his chin. A blemish wouldn't spoil his mood. Today, he and the rest of Buttonwood Middle School were heading to Recode Global, a super-secretive high-tech company that was opening its doors to the public for the first time. Its megaplex of futuristic buildings was located on the outskirts of town, surrounded by invisible electric fences and security drones. The place always made Jason wonder, *What was Recode Global up to?*

1

Jason's own mom, Dr. Shannon Elaine Pascal, was one of Recode's top employees. Dr. Pascal called herself a scientist, but thanks to confidentiality agreements, she couldn't give Jason specific details about her work. All he could gather from her long-winded science-y explanations was that Recode Global used technology "to solve humanity's most vexing problems." The only other clues he had about her job lay in her home office, an underground laboratory specially built for Dr. Pascal's tinkering. It was full of electronic equipment, tools, and techy parts, but she never let Jason in on what the stuff was for. Building tiny robots that could perform life-saving micro-surgeries on sick people? Was she working on space tech to colonize another planet in the event of a global warming crisis? His mother couldn't possibly be *that* cool—or could she?

Jason headed downstairs for breakfast, taking the stairs two at a time. The TV in the kitchen reported the morning news. Today would be sunny and clear, with a high of 77. *Perfect.*

He entered the kitchen and found his dad, Ray Pascal, sitting at the breakfast table, staring intently at the TV mounted on the wall. A poufy-haired anchorwoman was talking about the upcoming meteor shower that would light up Earth's sky.

"Where's Mom?" Jason said as he took a seat beside his dad at the table.

Ray held up a finger to quiet Jason.

Jason watched the TV.

"Don't forget to mark your calendars," the anchorwoman said. "Comet Swift-Tuttle is on its way. Get to Presidio Park next weekend for the best viewing!"

Jason's dad turned to Jason. "We have to see that. Your mother would love it."

"Yeah, Dad," Jason agreed. "Sounds cool." Though he could think of a billion other things that would be more interesting than staring at a black sky, looking for itty-bitty flashing stars. "Speaking of Mom, where is she?"

"Already at the office," Ray replied. "Your mother said everyone had to go in early. Your field trip is a major event." He slid an empty bowl over to Jason and waggled a box of Choco Crunch.

Jason grabbed the box and poured himself a bowl of cereal. "Dad, what are they going to show us? Are we going to watch scientists whisper to each other or what?" He scooped up a spoonful of cereal and shoved it in his mouth. *Yum.* No need for milk.

His father chuckled. "I only know a little about what they're cooking up, but I bet by the end of the day you'll think Recode is more *off the chain* than my bikes." He elbowed Jason. "Get it? Off the chain?"

Jason groaned. Ray Pascal owned Spokes, a bicycle shop a few miles from their house. While Jason's mom loved everything science, his dad loved bikes and, unfortunately, bike jokes.

Ray got up from the table, taking his bowl with him. "Also, your mom said they're providing lunch and treats like cupcakes—you can't go wrong."

"Cupcakes?" Jason smiled at the magic word, then shoved another spoonful of cereal into his mouth. He wondered what his mother was going to show everyone that could save the world.

The school bus went through one checkpoint after another. Jason and his classmates' excitement was palpable. "Wow!" a kid said. "Look at that!" Everyone pressed their faces against the windows for a better look. Finally, Jason could see Recode Global's buildings. With all that shiny glass and sleek metal, Recode looked like it had been ripped right out of a superhero movie. The buildings weren't tall, but the angles and curves of some of the structures seemed to defy gravity. Even the sculptures dotting the landscape could have passed as futuristic robots or objects designed by very talented aliens.

Jason's excitement doubled when he noticed a bunch of brightly colored food trucks and commercial vans flanking one side of a building—Tic-Tock-Thai, Bakin' With Bacon, Sugar-N-Spice . . . *oh yeah.*

Their bus pulled up alongside others, and students formed lines to be led into the building. As Jason surveyed the scene, he realized his dad was right. This was a *major* event. There were news crews everywhere. An older-looking man wearing a white lab coat talked into about five microphones at the same time while cameras rolled. The man gestured as he spoke, causing his crazy, Einstein-ish gray hair to wiggle with each motion.

As everyone got off the bus, Recode security guards made each student pass through security gates, then waved small credit-card-sized devices over each student. To Jason, it looked like his mom's company wasn't taking any chances. Every once in a while, a card would light up, and someone had to give up what they had, even *gum*, but oddly, everyone was allowed to keep their phones. After security checks were completed, one guard gave another a signal, and the mirrored double doors to Recode Global slowly slid open.

Jason and his class entered a great hall the size of a football field. The walls, ceiling, and floor were made of a smooth, silvery material. There was no furniture, decorations, or visible light fixtures—only wide-open space, clean surfaces, and a warm glow filling the vast area. A few students tried to snap pictures of the amazing nothingness with their phones, but complaints quickly filled the room.

"Hey, how come my phone doesn't work?"

"Mine won't power on."

"Same with me!"

Jason pulled his own phone from his pocket. The screen was dark, and he couldn't turn it on. *Creepy.*

A soothing female voice filled the room. "Welcome, students. Please note, photography is prohibited. Your cellular devices have been temporarily disabled."

"Kinda spooky," a girl murmured beside him.

Jason turned to look at who was talking. She had long black hair, brown eyes, and a slightly pointy chin. She was wearing a T-shirt with an image of Princess Leia on it that read *A WOMAN'S PLACE IS IN THE RESISTANCE.* "You're Jason, right?" she asked.

Before Jason could answer, the girl went on. "My mom said your mom actually works here. I just moved a few doors down from you, so hello, neighbor!" She smiled. "I'm Maya Mateo."

Jason smiled back. "Hi."

"So, what's your mom going to show us?"

"Uh . . . honestly, I have no idea." Jason hoped it didn't involve flowcharts and diagrams. His mother was particularly good at those.

5

Maya looked around the room as the rest of their schoolmates filed in. "Looks like she has a neat job. My dad's an airline pilot, a lot less fancy than this."

Just as Maya started to say something else, another female voice boomed all around them. "*Are you ready for the future?!*"

Everyone yelled in agreement.

Maya leaned in closer so Jason could hear. "Your dad owns Spokes, right? Can you meet me there tomorrow at one? I need to fix my bike."

"Sure," Jason said, even though his dad did all the fixing at the shop. Still, he hoped he could be useful to Maya. She seemed like the coolest neighbor he'd ever had. *Star Wars* and bikes? Sure beat Mrs. McGuffin and her snarling cats.

"People, I didn't hear you," the voice said, growing louder. "*Are you ready for the future?*"

Jason's whole body vibrated from the volume. He joined everyone else in shouting, "Yes!"

"Then welcome to Recode Global, where the future is *now*."

Suddenly, the lights went out.

The room was pitch black.

"Was that supposed to happen?" Maya said.

"I have no idea." Jason couldn't see a thing!

"What's going on?" came another confused voice.

As if to answer the question, a burst of electronic sounds filled the room, like a techno dance song. Multicolored waves of light pulsed through the air, and the crowd whooped to the music. Jason started to wonder if they had gone to a nightclub instead of a field trip. A velvety female voice emanated from all around. "You are in a place of imagination and wonder!" A circle of light appeared on the ceiling. As Jason's eyes adjusted, a woman dressed in all black, like Catwoman, descended out of the darkness on a disc-shaped hoverboard.

The disc zoomed through the air without visible rotors or jets to keep it aloft. Instead, a pair of metallic, Frisbee-sized circles from its underside crackled with bluish-white electricity. The vehicle lowered to a platform that rose up as if the floor was changing shape to give her a landing spot. The woman stepped off the disc and onto the platform. She put her hands on her hips like a true superhero.

Everyone erupted into applause.

"My name is Ula Varner," the woman said, "I'm the public relations director for Recode Global." She tapped her belt, and her all-black outfit turned sky blue. Students gasped with awe.

"If only my mom knew to shop where she does," Maya commented.

"We have gathered here the brightest, most future-literate people in the world," Ula continued. "They come from more than 100 countries all over the planet. They are physicists, geneticists, biologists, material scientists, and engineers. Our mission is to reimagine the operating systems of life to ensure the sustainability of humankind. Recode Global is here to recode the world!"

Everyone clapped again.

"You've already had a glimpse of what we are doing to accomplish that," Ula continued. "Metamaterials for our modular, malleable floor; chroma-shifting fabrics for my versatile outfit; and new transportation like the ODSCIP." She gestured to the flying hoverboard. "The

Omni-Directional Super-Conducting Platform! That's three new technologies already. Wait until you see what's next!"

Another round of applause sounded through the room.

The ODSCIP flew up and away, and the hall filled with a soft white light. "Come this way," Ula said.

Everyone was led toward a wall that melted away to form an opening. Weirdly, there were no seats in the space within. Ushers guided the group toward spots on the floor, and Maya was directed to the opposite side of the room with her class. "Catch ya later, Jason," she said.

Jason nodded goodbye as an usher organized his class into neat rows. The room darkened. The walls, ceiling, and floor seemed to transform into fields of stars, but it was way better than any planetarium Jason had ever visited. Everything seemed so . . . real. It was like he was suspended in outer space. He reached out to a nearby star. It pulsed from his touch.

"Greetings," a male voice said. "It won't be long before we can live on other planets, even vacation in outer space." As the narrator spoke, planets and asteroids zoomed in and out of view. Then Jason saw floating translucent images against the starry backdrop. People boarded spaceships and landed on faraway planets. These "tourists" then shuttled around in rover-like vehicles from craters to mountains to planetary oceans as easily as if they were visiting a place like Hawaii to see the sights. "These grand visions are closer to reality than you think," the narrator continued. "As you tour Recode Global, prepare to be astonished. What you will see today is only the beginning."

The group was led through another melting wall into a large space where a man dressed in a white button-down and jeans waited on a platform. He rolled up a shirt sleeve to reveal a gleaming prosthetic. "I lost my arm in combat three years ago," he explained as he held out his arm and wiggled his fingers. "But now, thanks to Recode Global, it's better than new!" The fingertips on his mechanical hand opened to reveal all sorts of tools, like a high-tech Swiss Army knife-hand.

Jason recognized a screwdriver, a mini flashlight, scissors, and . . . a laser pointer?

The man aimed the finger at a blank white wall, and a beam of red light shot out. He used it to burn a large smiley face into the wall. It wasn't just a laser pointer; it was a *laser*. "Harmless against humans," he said, "so long as you don't look at it directly."

A few students gasped.

The man laughed. "*Kidding!*"

The group continued onward, moving from room to room. Jason was riveted by mind-blowing displays and demonstrations: exoskeletons that enabled people to outrun cheetahs and lift things as heavy as elephants, giant trees that had been engineered to grow into actual treehouses—a product of something called synthetic biology—and nano-sized medical robots that could clear clogged arteries, destroy cancer cells, and knit fractured bones together.

Lunch featured a panel presentation, hosted by a couple of robot comedians who weren't all that funny. Perhaps teaching computers how to make jokes was still a work in progress. Then the students were herded into a lecture hall with a movie-theater-sized screen.

Jason slid into a modern desk with built-in surfaces that allowed everyone to take notes using touchscreens. While people sat down, Jason spotted his mom onstage. Finally, Dr. Shannon Elaine Pascal was on.

Dr. Pascal smoothed the pockets of her white lab coat. A stray lock of her brown hair had fallen into her glasses. Jason thought she looked positively tiny in a lecture hall filled with so many curious students.

The room finally settled down, and Dr. Pascal began.

"Students," Dr. Pascal said, "I have a problem for you to solve." She clicked a laser pointer in her hand and an equation appeared on a giant screen: "HI + AI = ?"

With a fingertip, Jason wrote the formula onto his screen.

$HI + AI =$

He drew a sad face and sighed. Leave it to his mom to turn everything into an equation.

No one attempted to answer the question.

"First, let's address HI," Dr. Pascal said. "It stands for human intelligence, an intelligence that is unparalleled by any other living species on Earth. Then there's AI. It stands for—"

"Artificial intelligence," a girl called out.

"Correct!" Dr. Pascal replied, her face lighting up.

Jason thought his mom was probably glad that at least one person was paying attention.

"When you combine HI and AI, you get . . ." Dr. Pascal clicked the pointer and the answer appeared.

$HI + AI = $ *The Future Today.*

"This powerful formula," Dr. Pascal said, "is our key to solving humanity's most challenging problems *now*."

Dr. Pascal dimmed the lights. As she spoke, images of the human brain and neural networks flashed on the screen. Then lines of programming code floated upward, followed by pictures of machines, computers, and smart devices used by people.

"Humanity working together with AI is already changing how we live," Dr. Pascal went on, "but in ways that go beyond what most people see."

Jason's mind began to wander, and he contemplated how awesome it would be if his mom wasn't just a theory person but actually built droids like the ones right out of *Star Wars*.

"To solve complex issues," Dr. Pascal said, "such as climate change, food shortages, and epidemics, we must learn how to re-engineer complex systems. But this has been hard to do with human intelligence alone. We need AI as a partner."

Then Jason's mom started using phrases like "artificial general intelligence," "deep tech," and "neural code" with sloping charts and graphs. This went on for several minutes, and Jason started to lose track; a kid in the row in front of him was doodling a picture of an army of aliens attacking a stick-figure version of a woman in a lab coat. *Not good.*

Jason's gaze wandered over to the caterers in back wearing Sugar-N-Spice T-shirts. They were setting up desserts on long tables. One caterer was massively built, making even Jason's towering dad look kind of average-sized. Jason worried his baseball-mitt hands might crush the dainty cupcakes he was setting out. Next to him, a blonde caterer with a streak of pink in her hair unloaded cookies and mini-cakes. The caterers watched Jason's mom as they worked. Maybe they found her confusing, too.

Suddenly all the lights in the room cut out. But this time, it didn't feel intentional.

"That's odd," Dr. Pascal commented in the dark. "Let's give this a second. No need to worry."

The lights came back on again.

Just when Jason thought his mother would continue, another Recode employee in a lab coat stepped onto the stage and whispered in his mother's ear.

"Students," Dr. Pascal announced, "I am so sorry, but I won't be able to finish my talk. If you could just follow your teacher's instructions to leave the building, that would be great." She gestured toward the exit on one side of the room.

Jason gaped from his seat. That was it? Did someone pull the plug on his mom's speech?

"Oh, and don't forget to pick up a Recode Global gift bag," Dr. Pascal continued. "Thank you for visiting."

Security officers immediately began ushering everyone out of the room. Jason heard one of them tell another, "We've got a Code 7."

Code 7?

Jason stared at his mother. He felt relieved that her presentation was over, but he was also ticked off that they had cut it short. His mother didn't look so happy either as she stepped off the stage.

Jason followed his teacher's instructions to line up to leave. The big dude and the pink-streak lady were putting all the goodies back into boxes. Recode wasn't going to bother letting everyone grab a snack? Jason's teacher handed him a Recode Global gift bag. He rummaged through it: Recode Global decals, pens, and a miniature of the ODSCIP. Not a single treat. The bag itself was a cool drawstring backpack. He slung it onto his back.

Dr. Pascal came over and took Jason aside. "I'm disappointed I couldn't finish my talk, Jason. We didn't even get to the part about how important it is to be future literate."

"I'm sad, too," Jason said. More for his mother though. "I heard a security guard say, 'Code 7.' What's that mean?"

His mother frowned. "No idea. There are some things here at Recode that even I'm not privy to." She glanced over her shoulder, then her face turned really serious. "I want you to truly understand what I do, though. Would you like that?"

"Wait, more charts?" *Umm—*

"This will be much better, I promise." She looked at him intently. "It will change how you view the world."

"Right now?" Jason noticed his class starting to leave. "Everyone's going."

"Listen, my boss and the rest of the team will be busy with press conferences all day." She scanned the room. "Really, it's now or never. They're clearing the room. When will I ever get a chance to have you here?"

Jason bit his lip. "Never?"

Dr. Pascal smiled. "Stay put. I'll let your teacher know that you're staying with me."

Jason had to hand it to his mother. She never gave up, and he *did* wonder what her office was like. Was it anything like her lab at home? Did people fly ODSCIPs to the water cooler? Would *he* get to ride one?

Dr. Pascal returned. "All set," she said. "It's time for you to meet my latest project. Trust me, Jason, you've never seen anything like it."

2

A GLITCHY DOOR AND A GIANT MONKEY JANITOR

Jason hurried to keep pace with his mother. They took a passage leading away from the news crews and Recode workers. He spotted a few security guards around the corner, but they looked busy guiding students out of the building.

"Stick close," Dr. Pascal said, "and don't touch anything, okay? I don't think it's *officially* forbidden to bring you upstairs, but it's not something I want to advertise."

Dr. Pascal led Jason to a pair of metal doors with a nickel-sized red sensor in front. There was a flash of light between the sensor and her eyes, and the doors opened.

Jason followed his mom into an elevator. When the doors to his mother's floor slid open, the office spaces looked average. Cubicles, offices, carpeting . . . no rising platforms, melting walls, or flying vehicles. "Where's all the fancy stuff, Mom?"

"The ground floor is for presentations and visitors," Dr. Pascal said. "It's the show—the wow factor. Upstairs is practical, more work-oriented. We have some meta-materials up here, too, but they're mostly in secured labs."

She led Jason to a thick glass door set in the middle of an equally thick glass wall. Another sensor flashed at her eyes before the door opened with a gentle *hiss*. Aside from the soft swishing of their feet on the carpet, all was quiet. They passed empty workspaces and offices. After two more security doors and a long corridor, Dr. Pascal pointed to a tidy room that had a desk and a swivel chair and lots of screens.

"That's my office, and my lab is across the hall. Now who will you tell about this?"

"Uh . . . nobody?"

"Right. Phone off, please."

"Mom, security took care of that earlier. My phone still doesn't work."

"Perfect." Dr. Pascal stopped in front of a plain white wall across from her office.

Jason gave her a confused look as she leaned forward toward a blank space on the wall, or, rather, blank except for a nickel-sized bump. There was another flash of light and a door-sized section of the wall slid open with a whispery *whoosh*.

Whoa. A secret door!

Dr. Pascal led Jason into a white space. A tall white cylinder stood in the center. "My lab is bullet-proof, fire-proof, and bomb-proof," she said. "It could survive the whole building collapsing." The door automatically closed behind them.

"Wait a second," Jason said. "Are you telling me people might blow up this place?"

Dr. Pascal laughed. "It's sweet you're concerned, but we are safe. The room is electromagnetically shielded, too, just in case there are any nefarious forces at work."

"Nefar—what? Speak English, Mom."

"You know, bad guys, Jason."

Jason frowned. "Like who?"

Dr. Pascal sighed. "We've been over this before, Jason. I don't know *who* the bad guys are exactly, but remember: technology is informed not only by science, but also by history. For centuries, we've known—"

Jason put his hand up. "Wait, I got it, Mom. For centuries, we've known that where there is good . . . there is evil."

"You have been paying attention."

Jason looked around some more. There were no decorations, no seats . . . what kind of secret lab was this? There was hardly anything to see. "So where is everything?"

"Display equipment," Jason's mom said.

Suddenly, the white walls became transparent and behind them was every kind of part and gadget imaginable—a scientist's dream. It was definitely a step up from Mom's home office.

"That's awesome," Jason said. "Now I get it."

Dr. Pascal gestured at the column. "This right here is the best part. My dear friend is inside. I must keep him isolated."

Jason eyed the column. "What kind of friend can you keep in a container without any air holes?"

"You'll see. At this stage of development, I have to do this. No radio or Internet. Nothing." Dr. Pascal leaned in for another eye scan in front of the cylinder. After a flash, its walls slid down, revealing—

"A smartwatch?" Jason stared at the dark face of a sleek-looking watch trimmed in silver metal. "Mom, hate to tell you this, but Apple already has you beat."

"He's not a smartwatch, Jason. He's a prototype of the world's most sophisticated artificial intelligence."

Jason walked around the cylinder as he stared at the device. The watch face began to glow blue. "So exactly how smart is it?"

"Actually, all smart devices you're familiar with aren't truly smart," Dr. Pascal explained. "At best, they can do calculations, run automated programs, and conduct other low-level processes. They have 'narrow intelligence'—they can *only* perform those tasks that humans program in response to specific events. However, Proto can think on his own, similar to the way that humans do. He's the type of AI that I brought up during my talk."

Jason noticed the watch was glowing softly in beats, like it was breathing. "Is Proto thinking now?"

"He is thinking constantly. Humans, together with technology like Proto, can assist in the design, build, and operation of the tech we develop here. All of those things we introduced today from exoskeletons to nanobots—"

"Wait, Proto helped build those things?" Jason couldn't believe it. His mom *was* working on something cool.

"Under very controlled circumstances," Dr. Pascal said. "Proto has been on our design teams and has already made significant contributions. We're just getting started, Jason. His possibilities could go beyond anything we know today."

Jason peered at the watch. "So how do you make this thing work?"

"I am not *this thing*," a soft male voice said. "My name is Proto, short for *prototype*."

Jason flinched with surprise. "Mom, it spoke!"

Dr. Pascal smiled. "Proto, this is my son, Jason. Jason, say hello."

"Hello," Jason said nervously. "Uh . . . how are you?"

"How am I?" Proto repeated. "That inquiry has multiple interpretations. Do you mean, how do I exist? Dr. Pascal created me. Do you mean, how am I composed? My external body is made of heat-resistant, shock-resistant, electrically insulated carbon nanotubes and transparent alumi—"

"Whoa," Jason said. "Usually the answer to that question is 'good' or 'not bad.'"

"I see," Proto said. "You meant, what is the state of my mental or physical health? Correct? Pardon my loquacity." The blue light flickered rapidly, accompanied by gentle, natural-sounding laughter, as natural as anything coming from a watch could sound.

"Um," Jason said. "Lo-what?"

"Loquacity. Definition: the quality of speaking superfluously." Proto paused. "Would you like a full analysis of the word's Latin origins?"

"No, that's okay."

"Socially speaking, Proto is young," Dr. Pascal said. "He's still working out how to interact with others. But he is a sharp listener and a good student."

"He does talk like a human," Jason remarked. "Sort of."

"Thank you," Proto said. "Sort of," he added.

Dr. Pascal smiled. "Yes, I designed Proto to learn how to be empathetic, too. He has chemical sensors, facial-recognition algorithms, and other bio-monitoring systems to help him read, understand, and relate to human emotions and situations. Amazing, right?"

Jason studied Proto more closely. "Yeah, amazing." He reached out to touch him. His mother quickly pulled his hand back. "Remember what I said, no touching. This is a billion-dollar device."

"$993,952,679.28 thus far to be exact," Proto said.

"Very good, Proto," Dr. Pascal. "But it may be considered boastful if you talk about how much you cost, so let's keep that information within Recode Global."

Proto's light blinked. "I do not understand. Jason does not belong to Recode Global. Only authorized Recode Global individuals are allowed into my chamber. Is my understanding incorrect?"

Jason looked from Proto to Dr. Pascal. His mom had just been called out by a super-intelligent watch!

"Uh, I'll explain later," Dr. Pascal stammered.

"Of course," Proto said sheepishly. "I have a remarkable neural network, but there are many gaps in my knowledge and experiences, particularly when it comes to human etiquette. That may be the source of my social awkwardness."

"Hey, there's nothing wrong with being socially awkward," Jason said. "Been there, done that."

"That's part of the reason we keep Proto isolated here," Dr. Pascal said. "If he becomes overstimulated with data, without proper guidance, I don't know what impact it would have on his development or what he might say unintentionally." She turned to Proto. "I only want what's best for you, and I promise you'll get to leave this room and experience a lot more when the time is right."

"When the time is right," Proto repeated. "Thank you." He paused. "I do not know what I can truly accomplish yet, but I am ready to learn."

Jason suddenly had a scary thought. "Mom, could I talk to you privately for a second?" He turned to Proto. "Human stuff. No offense."

"No offense taken," Proto said. "I have plenty of 'wrist-watch-computer-stuff' I can do in the meantime."

"Now that was kinda funny," Jason said. "See you real soon, Proto."

"See you real soon," Proto repeated.

Dr. Pascal closed Proto into his cylinder. "What's up?"

"I didn't want to offend Proto, but . . ." Jason paused. "Mom, this is starting to feel like one of those movies where the robots get so smart, they take control of everything."

Dr. Pascal smiled. "Honey, Proto has programming to guide him, yes, but I also gave him ethical heuristics. Unlike the machines in those types of stories, he wasn't built with confusing commands that might cause dangerous logical conflicts. Proto's main governing principle is to work *with* humanity, not against it."

Jason raised an eyebrow. "So the only danger is he talks us to death. Are you sure?"

His mother laughed. "Trust me, Jase. Proto will help usher in the brightest possible future."

Jason tried to relax. His mother was almost always right, except for the time she washed a red sweater with all of his underwear, and everything came out pink. "But if there's a robot uprising, I get to say I told you so."

"It's a deal." Dr. Pascal glanced at her watch. "I better see Dr. Cooper now. He wanted me to check in with him.

Maybe it has something to do with what just happened during my presentation."

They left the lab and the door closed. Dr. Pascal waved Jason into her office. "Do you see why what I do is so important now?"

"I do. Will I be able to see Proto again? I can teach him how to reprogram my P.E. teacher."

Dr. Pascal laughed. "Proto will do no such thing. I have to go. You stay here. I'll be back soon."

As Dr. Pascal walked away down the corridor, Jason noticed the cushy spinning chair behind his mother's desk. It looked too comfortable to resist. Just as he was about to shrug off his gift bag and hop in for a good spin, he heard a familiar whispery *whoosh*. It sounded exactly like the opening and closing of Proto's shielded room.

Jason poked his head out of his mom's office. Sure enough, the hidden door in the wall was open. The opening was narrow, but Jason had sworn the door had closed behind them. This wasn't good; his mom could get into trouble if Proto got out. Jason debated whether he should wait in his mother's office as instructed or try to figure out how to close the door himself.

Hmm. He looked both ways before he stepped out of his mother's office. The coast was clear. He hurried over to the open wall-door, but he couldn't see the cylinder through the gap to know if Proto was okay. He decided he had to go in. He slipped through the gap in the doorway and gasped. He was staring at an empty cylinder. Proto wasn't there.

"Proto?" he whispered.

"Yes, Jason?" Proto said from the floor.

"Shhhh!" Jason said. "Whisper! Are you able to whisper?"

"Of course," Proto said in a remarkably human-sounding whisper. "Is this a game we are playing? I have never modulated my voice in this fashion."

"It's not a game," Jason said. "How did you get on the floor? It could be bad if someone sees you there. Did you open the door?"

"Addressing your questions in order," Proto said. "First, please allow me to demonstrate the function of my retractable legs—"

"*Proto*," Jason loud-whispered. "We don't have time to goof around. The door issue is important. Did you open it?"

"No," Proto said. "My cylinder and the door opened. Did Dr. Pascal initiate these activities?"

"I don't think so. She's not even here!"

Proto's light glowed brighter. "Then they must be controlled by some other mechanism of which I am unaware. Would you like me to try to determine how to operate them?"

"You can do that?"

"I do not know. I am designed to learn, but I cannot guarantee success at this task."

Just then Jason heard a faint, familiar *hiss*, like the big glass security doors opening. "Wait!" He cocked his head toward the door. "Is that my mom?"

Proto's blue light flickered for a moment. "My auditory sensors have verified the opening and closing of two sliding partitions farther down the hall. I am also able to detect various biorhythms indicating a human being currently heading in this direction. It is difficult to get an exact reading at this distance, but based on respiratory patterns, rate of stride, and foot impacts on the flooring, I believe this is an adult male human or, perhaps, an unusually large male chimpanzee walking upright. It is not, however, your mother."

"I gotta get out of here so I don't get into trouble. Stay out of sight until the coast is clear."

"To which coast are you referring?" Proto asked. "Eastern U.S., Western U.S., African—"

"No, I mean, just hurry and get back in the cylinder."

Suddenly, Proto's wristwatch band split into eight metallic legs, making him look like a robotic spider with a glowing blue body. He jumped effortlessly from the floor to the cylinder.

Jason paused for a moment to take in Proto's Transformer-like abilities. *Cool.* He wondered what else Proto could do.

"You are studying me quite intently," Proto whispered. "Is there something wrong with me?"

"The correct question is," Jason said, "what *isn't* wrong with you?" He rushed over to the open gap. "Wait here a few seconds."

"I will wait here a few seconds," Proto whispered.

Jason crouched down by the open door and slowly poked his head out.

"Do your sensors detect the approaching primate?" Proto whispered.

"What? My *sensors?*" Jason glanced back at Proto. "Eyes and ears, Proto. But no, it's a long, twisty hallway. I probably won't see the guy until he's right here." Jason paused. "But for now, stay out of sight."

"For now, I shall stay out of sight."

"Don't worry," Jason said. "We can hang out later."

"By hanging out, do you mean—"

"Shhh! Please stay quiet and don't tell anyone we even had this conversation, or we'll get into trouble."

Proto said nothing in response. Instead, he blinked his blue eye-light.

"Perfect. See you soon!" Jason slipped through the opening again, pausing in the doorway to double-check that the hall was still clear. He took a deep breath, then dashed into his mother's office.

He heard the nearest security door hiss open and then close. The mystery person had to be close now. Jason ducked behind his mom's desk, but unfortunately that meant he couldn't see who was coming. The footsteps swished ever closer on the carpet. Jason held his breath as the man whistled some random tune.

The footsteps paused near his mom's office. He heard a rustling sound like a trash can being shaken as though someone were emptying it. *All that over a janitor?*

Then, after what felt like the longest seconds ever, the footsteps went back the way they came. Jason waited until he heard the security door open and close again. There was another whispery *whoosh*. Jason peeked around the desk. The wall-door had closed as mysteriously as it had opened. *Weird.* Maybe the door was glitchy, or maybe Proto had figured out how to close it?

Jason finally got out from under the desk, slipped off the Recode gift bag, and plopped into his mother's chair. The office seemed quiet again. A few minutes later, Jason heard more doors opening and closing, but this time he could tell it was his mother by the sound of her shoes on the flooring. Those were definitely her light footsteps. Maybe Proto had already taught him something about paying attention. Sure enough, his mother appeared in her office doorway.

"Hey, hon, sorry about the delay," Dr. Pascal said. "I'm afraid I have bad news. I have to go to a conference in Geneva, of all places." She set her tablet on her desk with a thud. "It's important." She sighed.

"How long will you be gone?" Jason said, not at all surprised. His mother often got called out for important meetings all over the globe.

"Dr. Cooper says it will be just a few days."

Jason smiled, glad that his mother was distracted by work. "No problem, Mom." He spun in her chair. "I figured out how fast I can swivel in this thing while you were gone." There was no need to tell her about the crazy door situation or his little unauthorized Proto-visit.

What good would it do to worry his mother over a glitchy door and a giant monkey janitor anyway?

IN NEED OF DESSERT

The next morning, Jason woke up in his usual Saturday style—late—and with a vague recollection of dreaming about an alien spider hopping around his bedroom. He went downstairs to guzzle some O.J. for breakfast and spotted a note on the kitchen counter.

Out to run some last-minute errands. Leaving for the airport in a few hours. Hope to see you before I go! Aunt Dotty will be staying over while I'm gone. Make sure you stay out of trouble while Dad's at the shop.

Love, Mom

Aunt Dotty? *Yes!* She made the best spaghetti ever.

Twenty minutes later, Jason was on his bike, blazing through the forest trails near his home to get to Spokes. He had an appointment to keep with his new friend and neighbor, Maya.

When he arrived, he skidded to a stop, throwing up a cloud of dust. He locked his bike to the rack next to another bike, a well-used MOBI Territory Trail XT. He did a double take. Jason almost didn't believe what he was seeing. The MOBI Territory was backordered for a full year, impossible to get. Who owned such a fine machine?

He popped into the graciously air-conditioned Spokes and noticed Maya right away. She was talking to his dad at the checkout counter, wearing a red backpack checkered with patches.

"Hey, Maya," Jason said as he approached her.

"Hey, Jason," Maya said cheerfully. "Thanks for meeting me. This is such a great place to shop!"

"It is an *excellent* place to shop," Ray Pascal said, obviously happy to have yet another local fan. "Hey Jase, did you know our new neighbor is into bikes?"

"Just found out yesterday," Jason said, wondering if his father would find a way to embarrass him. "What do you need for your bike, Maya?" Jason walked down an aisle of bike accessories, *away* from his father. "A new bell? Streamers?"

"Streamers?" Maya laughed. She followed him past an enormous array of bike tires and chains. "Nope, I snapped a peg on my MOBI the other day." She gestured to the window toward the rack outside. "I bent a couple of spokes, and I'm always on the lookout for new decals."

"Wait a second," Jason said. "That's *yours*?" He called to his father, "Dad, we've got a 218 and a 230 outside, rack slot number 3. It's a MOBI. Be good to it."

His father gave him a funny look. It was usually Jason's dad who barked orders at Jason, not the other way around. But he played along anyway. "I'm on it, Jase."

Maya tossed him her bike-lock key.

"I'll show you what we've got for tricking out your bike," Jason said.

"Awesome," Maya said. "Cool field trip yesterday, right?"

"Definitely." Jason thought about Proto. "AI is crazy stuff, huh?"

"I thought your mom did such a great job explaining it."

Jason fought to keep his face neutral. *She did?*

"How close is she to having a working prototype?" Maya asked. "I wondered if she was going to put all that brain power into a robot or something."

Jason almost laughed at how *beyond* close she was and wondered if Maya would think Proto was as cool as he did. Surely she would. He wished he could tell her about Proto.

Instead he changed the subject. "How about I show you some great gadgets for your bike." He gestured at the wall of accessories in front of them. "Speedometer . . . odometer . . . a waterproof, shock-protected phone-mount for your handlebars. Have you ever taken a vid with your phone while you ride? That's the best."

"Got that covered," she said. "I never leave home without my DronePro. It records my best rides."

Jason looked at her as though she came from a distant highly advanced planet. "You have a DronePro?" He could already tell they would get along just fine. Especially if she would let him borrow her gear. "Impressive."

"Miss Maya," Ray said, carrying her MOBI inside with one hand like it was a toy. "Your bike will be ready in a few."

"Thanks, Mr. Pascal," she said.

"Anything else?" Jason's dad said as he set up the bike for repair.

She pulled a decal of an angry-looking bulldog off the wall. "I'll take this one. I've always had a fondness for the misunderstood."

Jason and Maya walked over to the register.

"Thank you, Mr. Pascal," Maya said as she paid. "Jason, do you have a DronePro, too?"

"Not yet." *Not ever.* His mom would never let him have one because she thought the giant company that made them wasn't *pro-social* and their privacy policies were absolutely demonic. Whatever that meant.

"You can try mine if you show me the best trails around here," Maya volunteered. "Deal?"

Jason smiled. "Deal."

After Maya left with her bike, Jason turned to his dad. "She's got a DronePro, Dad. So unfair."

"That's your mom's rule, Jase. She won't even let me carry them in the store, so I have to sell number two in the market, and let me tell you, the BanditBat is not anywhere close to the Pro."

"Aw, man," Jason said. "Why is it always an evil conspiracy theory with Mom?" *Are there really people out there seeking world domination and ruining it for everyone else?*

Jason left the store, thinking about Maya and her awesome contraband, the DronePro. He unlocked his bike, tugged his helmet back on, then slipped on his sunglasses before pedaling toward the forest. Nothing made him feel better than a good ride. Jason aimed for a narrow dirt trail between two trees. A soft voice grabbed his attention. "If you'd like, *I* can record this ride for you."

Startled, Jason whipped his head around. "Who said that?" It sounded like . . . "*Proto?*"

"Yes?"

Jason looked down at the handlebars of this bike. Proto was wrapped around the gearshift.

"I know you asked me to be quiet yesterday," Proto said, "but after you expressed an interest in capturing your ride on video, I wanted to offer assistance."

Jason merely stared, stunned. Proto was not supposed to be out here!

"Proto!" Jason gasped at last. "What are you doing here?"

"I am speaking to you, Jason. Here."

"No, I mean, where were you hiding all this time?"

"Your pocket."

"My *pocket?*" Jason patted the other pouches on his cargo shorts, fearing what else he'd find. "You were in there this whole time?"

"Only since you left your room this morning," Proto said.

"But you were supposed to stay in your column-thingy at Recode!"

"I did, and then you specifically requested I stay out of sight."

Jason squinted at Proto. "Yeah, so?"

"Perhaps I need to go over the order of your requests again." Proto squinted back in his own way by narrowing his blue glow to a thin pinpoint of light. "You asked me to stay in my columnar home, which I did, and then you next asked me to remain out of sight, which I also did by hiding in your gift bag. You told me to stay quiet as well in between those requests and I followed each instruction precisely. However, you did not tell me how long I should remain quiet, so I had to make an estimation based on my clear mission to help humanity, which

I reasoned included you when you had a distinct desire to video rides using a DronePro."

Jason shook his head. "What am I going to do now, Proto?" His mom could totally get fired if anyone knew he had Proto.

"Allow me to help," Proto said. "To video your ride—"

"That's not what I meant, Proto. You're not supposed to be out of the lab. Mom could get into trouble, and so could I. Recode will think we stole you!"

Proto's light pulsed as though he was processing something deeply. "I apologize for any misunderstanding. It is possible my sudden exposure to this outside world is causing me to not function as intended. Dr. Pascal warned me of this."

"We have to get you back," Jason said, "it's Saturday. Do Recode people work with you on weekends? Maybe Mom can get you back to the lab without anyone knowing you've been gone."

"No, I do not believe any visits are scheduled for this weekend."

Jason checked the time on his phone. "We better hurry before Mom leaves for the airport. Jump in my pocket and hide."

"Wait!" Proto's blue glow began to flash rapidly as if he were expressing happiness. "I don't need to hide. I can disguise myself to avoid visual detection. Dr. Pascal has taught me this already." He crawled off the handlebar and wrapped himself around Jason's wrist. Instead of a dark face, Proto now displayed a digital watch face that looked just like an Ironman sports watch. "How do you like me now?"

"Great, let's go," Jason said. "If I take the shortest trail, it should only take twenty minutes."

"Twenty minutes is not necessary," Proto replied. "By my calculations, I can get you there far sooner than that."

"How do you know that?"

"That was simple to ascertain," Proto said, "Google Earth is quite useful. I was able to access their database via the Internet while I was in your room last night. Then I realized that if I combine the images with my GPS, I can gain many useful insights."

Proto flashed again with excitement. "Allow me to demonstrate. First you will need an earpiece, so you can hear me better as I help you find your way back with maximum efficiency." He reached inside his watch body to reveal a small, soft piece of tan material.

Jason took the earpiece from Proto. It fit easily into Jason's ear canal. "It's not too bad. Kinda squishy."

"It molds itself to your ear canal from the heat of your body." Proto's voice came through crystal clear in Jason's ear. "Now wear your sunglasses."

"Why?"

"I have identified at least fourteen reasons why humans should wear sunglasses. Would you like to hear them all?"

"Oh, never mind, Proto." Jason put on his sunglasses. "Now can we leave?"

"Let's begin with the landscape," Proto said, "so I can orient you to the journey we are about to make."

Jason gasped as his view changed. Proto projected topographical images for every nearby dirt trail. It was so totally Tony Stark! "Cool. Now I get it."

"I recommend this path," Proto said, highlighting a path that wasn't a forest preserve trail. It cut through streams, went up and down ravines, through a small river . . .

It looked positively . . . *"Fun!"* Jason said.

"Follow my precise instructions, and you will get there in nine minutes and fifteen seconds."

"Let's do this." Jason pushed off.

Proto guided him through inclines and declines, highlighting hard-to-see roots and rocks.

"Watch out for the rabbit, Jason," Proto warned.

"Got it!" Jason flew over a log and sailed over a surprised bunny's ears.

"Now cycle faster, Jason, you will need to achieve a minimum sped of 18.3 miles per hour."

Jason pumped his legs faster. He saw an upcoming stream that was at least fifteen feet wide below a ravine. "Should I turn or what?"

"Go straight and *faster*, Jason."

"Straight? But—"

"Faster, Jason! The shortest distance between two points is—"

"—a straight line!" Jason gripped the handlebars and pushed harder through the trees. The trees broke away to reveal a clear sky above and a babbling stream below as Jason and his bike sailed across the ravine and landed on the other side.

"That was awesome!"

"One more obstacle, Jason. Please maintain your speed."

This time, Jason whooped as he scaled a natural rock formation and took a big jump off. He got enough airtime to twist his bike halfway around before righting himself and landing perfectly on the other side.

"I'd never have made that without you!" Jason said.

When they reached the border between the forest and the Pascals' property, Jason stopped the bike, exhausted.

"Nine minutes and fifteen seconds," Proto said. "As predicted."

Yes! Now they could get Proto back to his mother. But just as Jason was about to ride out to the field between the forest and his house, he noticed a black cargo van parked in his driveway. A Recode Global logo was emblazoned on the truck's side. *Wait a second.*

Jason swallowed. "Are we too late?"

"It appears that way," Proto said, a sad note to his voice.

Jason suddenly had the urge to run to the house and fess up about what had happened, but just then, the front door to his home opened, and a huge man stepped out. He was pulling his mom's rolling luggage. The pink-streaked blonde lady came out, followed by Dr. Pascal. She shut the door and followed them to the van.

Jason tilted his head. "That's weird. I've seen those two before, Proto. They're the Sugar-N-Spice caterers from Recode." Except now they were in just regular clothes. "Why would Mom be with a bunch of caterers?"

Proto's light dimmed. "One moment while I come up with a range of hypotheses."

The van door slid open and Dr. Pascal and the lady climbed in. The giant man sat in the front passenger seat and put on his sunglasses. Jason couldn't see the driver of the van.

"Are they like undercover security guards for Recode and not really cupcake caterers?" Jason proposed. "Could that be it?"

"This is possible," Proto said. "But I have another more likely explanation for this turn of events."

"What's that?" Jason said.

"Your mother could simply be in need of dessert."

35

WHERE THERE IS GOOD

"I have an idea." Jason pulled his phone from his pocket. "I'll call her and see what's up. If she acts funny, I'll know something is wrong."

"I see," Proto said. "If Dr. Pascal tells us a joke, we will know she is all right."

Jason ignored Proto and put the call through. It went to voicemail. That wasn't good. He tried texting her a message that sounded natural. *Where are you? I'm home.*

He waited a few seconds. No reply.

"I'll call Dad," Jason said to himself.

Ray Pascal answered. "Hey, Jase. Everything okay? Shop's really busy. Can't really chat."

"Wait, Dad," Jason said. "I got home and saw Mom leaving in a Recode Global van. Did something happen with work?" *Like . . . has she been accused of major theft? Is she being taken in for investigation by strange cupcake people?*

"Oh yes," his father said. "Mom just messaged me and said United cancelled her flight, so she had to rush to catch an earlier flight. Recode sent a company car to get her there."

So the Sugar-N-Spice people *weren't* really caterers.

"Oh . . ." Jason's voice trailed off. Just then, a text notification came in on his phone.

"Buddy," Jason's dad said, "I gotta get back to work. I'm three customers deep, okay?"

"Yeah, see you later." Jason opened the new message. It was from his mother.

Hey, darling. Flight cancelled. Trying to catch an earlier one. Sorry no proper goodbye. Love you!

"I guess Mom's okay." Jason slipped the phone back into his pocket, even though he still had a weird feeling about the whole thing.

"Your friend Maya is approaching," Proto said into his ear.

"What, right now?" Jason asked, forgetting to whisper. "Where is she?"

"Hey there!" Maya suddenly appeared in front of him on her bike. She slowed to a stop. "I thought that was you. Are you coming back from a ride?"

"Yeah . . . uh . . . What are you doing here?"

She adjusted her backpack. "I live around here, remember? Was going to take my DronePro for a flight now that my bike is fixed."

"Right," Jason said.

She paused for a second and studied him up and down. "You okay?"

"Oh, yeah, fine," he said.

"Jason," Proto whispered in his ear, "you are not fine. My sensors detect biological indicators of elevated stress."

"Shhhh!"

"Huh?" Maya said. "I didn't say anything."

"No, just . . . shhhhure is nice out. That's what I meant."

"Yeah, beautiful."

Awkward silence.

"Perhaps she can be of some assistance," Proto said in Jason's ear.

Maya was looking right at Jason, and she'd surely notice if he whispered a response. He shook his head subtly, hoping to silence Proto. But the head-shake was apparently too subtle for Proto.

"Are you sure you're okay?" Maya said. "I think I just saw you twitch. Do you need me to go?"

"No . . . uh, wait," Jason blurted. He tried to think.

"Jason, did you hear me?" Proto asked.

Jason coughed and tried to say, "Quit it," at the same time. It didn't work.

"Jason?" Proto said, "has your vocal output been impaired? This is not good. Has something happened to your auditory capabilities?" Proto paused. "Have *I* damaged your hearing?"

"*Proto, be quiet!*" Jason hissed.

Proto stopped talking, but Maya was now staring at Jason with pursed lips and an arched eyebrow.

"Did you just call me 'Toto'?" Maya asked.

"Uh, no, I was talking to . . . myself?" Jason squeaked.

"Ohhhh-kay, whatever you say, Jason." Maya made a move to get back on her bike. "I guess I'll let you talk to yourself then."

Jason wanted to tell Maya what he knew. "No, stop. I need to talk to you." Maybe Proto was right. She *might* be able help. He had no idea what to do about the caterers or Proto. Just then, a couple cycling together approached the trail entrance. Then a neighbor started to mow her lawn.

"We shouldn't stand here," Jason said. *Too many people.* "Follow me."

Maya didn't budge. "Why should I?"

"Because I need your help," Jason said seriously.

Maya stared at him a moment longer.

Jason gave her a pleading look. "Come on, Maya."

"Something's really wrong, isn't it?"

Jason nodded.

"Fine." Maya rolled her bike as Jason led her to his house. "This better be good."

They put their bicycles in Jason's garage.

"Wait right here," Jason said. Before he let Maya into the house, he went inside to give it a quick once-over. No one was in the kitchen, living room . . . nobody upstairs. He came back down. Everything seemed normal.

"Come in." Jason led Maya into the living room through the kitchen. He began to draw all the window shades.

"You're starting to creep me out," Maya said. "What's going on?"

"I want to take a few precautions, that's all." Jason pulled down another shade. "Promise me you won't tell anyone?"

Maya stared hard at him, like she was debating if she wanted to cut and run or stay put. Finally, she sighed, took her backpack off, and set it on the couch. She plopped down beside it. "I promise."

Jason joined Maya on the couch. Where could he start without sounding like a crazy person? "Okay, remember my mom's talk about humanity collaborating with artificial intelligence?"

"Yeah."

Jason pointed to the glowing blue device on his wrist. "This is what she meant. Proto, say hello to Maya."

"Jason," Proto hissed into his ear, "why are you telling her about *me?* I asked *you* to ask for her help."

"I am, but she needs to know. It's okay. I promise, Proto."

"Very well, Jason."

Maya glared at Jason. "Are you still talking to me . . . or you . . . or who? You have to cut that out!"

"Maya, I'm serious." Jason put Proto close to her face. "This is my mom's invention."

"You expect me to believe your Timex Ironman is your mom's latest invention?"

"Did you hear that, Jason?" Proto said aloud. He unraveled from Jason's wrist and crawled up his arm to rest on Jason's shoulder. "She believed I was an ordinary time-telling device!"

"Holy cow!" Maya said, leaning back. "What is that thing?"

"Why is everyone calling me a thing, Jason?" Proto said. "I am—"

"An AI!" Maya said, "in a tiny robot body. Of course! Wow! Dr. Pascal invented this?"

"His name is Proto," Jason said.

"Umm . . . nice to meet you, Proto," Maya said.

Proto's glow blinked. "*Enchanté.* I am finding the French language to be fascinating."

"You're learning French?" Maya asked. "Like right now?"

"*Oui.* YouTube has wonderful tutorials."

"So you're surfing the Internet as we speak?" Maya's eyes widened. "That's incredible. Jason, how come we didn't see Proto at Recode Global?"

"See, that's the thing," Jason said, "we weren't supposed to." He filled Maya in on what had happened, giving her a quick version of how he met Proto, Proto's own little field trip out of his chamber, how he wasn't supposed to be here, and then his mother running off with Recode caterers.

"I knew there was something up with King Kong and Pinky," Maya said. "I noticed them, too."

"How?"

"I dunno. Call it women's intuition. That King Kong guy was staring at your mom in a way that would totally make me uncomfortable. And I overheard Pinky telling him to knock it off when they were cleaning up."

Jason shuddered. "Maybe Mom *is* in trouble. Maybe they think Mom has Proto. Proto, were you able to detect if she was in distress?"

"I'm so happy that you asked," Proto replied. "Allow me to be of assistance again. May I show you the video I recorded?"

"What? You recorded the whole thing?"

"Yes I did," Proto said. "It's an important part of how I learn." A moment later, Proto began projecting footage as a three-dimensional hologram right above the coffee table. *Whoa.* There they were, not quite life-sized since King Kong would likely hit the ceiling. Proto played back the moment King Kong and Pinky were escorting his mother out of the house.

"Upon further examination," Proto said as he zoomed in on Dr. Pascal's face, "her pupils are dilated beyond the average circumference that I normally measure when we are working together. That could be an indication of distress."

"That's not good." Jason paced the floor. "Maybe we should we call the police."

"And tell them what?" Maya said. "Your mother looks like she willingly walked off with her Recode co-workers here. That's all this video shows. And how could we possibly explain that we have Proto without landing ourselves in jail?"

True. Jason reached out and put his hand through the image of the van. "Is it possible this isn't really a Recode vehicle? Like, they disguised their catering van?"

"That is an interesting hypothesis," Proto said. He projected a blue arrow onto the image. "If you look here, we can see the Recode Global logo is an imperfectly applied decal. If we zoom in closer, I can detect that there is another label beneath the Recode Global one. This might be too subtle for human eyesight. Allow me to enhance the image." Proto replaced the regular-vision image with a projection of his observation. The Sugar-N-Spice logo hovered overhead.

"The van *isn't* Recode Global then," Maya said. "Proto, do you have facial recognition capabilities?"

"Of course," Proto said. "Dr. Pascal uses it to verify her identity when she must access my control system."

"Can you match the faces of these caterers to their identities?" Maya said. "And what about the driver?"

Proto fast-forwarded the video and stopped at a still image of the van backing down the driveway.

Jason hadn't seen the driver until now. He had been texting his mom at that moment. The driver looked like a regular middle-aged dude wearing a baseball cap low over his face. "I can't tell who that guy is. Can you, Maya?"

She shook her head.

Proto blinked for a moment. "I can attempt to identify all unknown persons in the vehicle with facial imagery. However, currently, I only have a visual inventory of some employees of Recode Global, the two of you, and other humans I have encountered while you and I were outside, plus the millions of faces I've seen on YouTube, but I do not know who those people are."

"We can fix that," Maya said, "since you have access to the Internet. Can you break into databases?"

"That would be against the law," Proto said. "I am not authorized to commit such an act according to federal and state laws unless ordered by a governmental body with such authority."

"Hmmm," Maya said, deep in thought. "Proto, access public records then for business registrations as Sugar-N-Spice *and* public criminal records—something tells me these guys might have had prior convictions."

Jason stared at Maya. "How do you know this? You sound like you could work for the FBI."

"My mom and I love to watch crime show reruns on the Mystery Channel."

"That explains it," Jason said. Proto was right to ask Maya for help.

"How long will a search take, Proto?" Maya asked.

Proto blinked. "I am finished. I found 5,043 business of the same name in the United States, including variant spellings and punctuation. However, there is no Sugar-N-Spice company operating in Buttonwood or the county. As for identifying the driver, no amount of enhancement will give me a clear picture of the driver's face, but I have discovered multiple image-matches on rap sheets for the other two people."

"Great!" Maya said.

"*Great?!*" Jason said. "How is my mom hanging with felons great?"

Maya suddenly looked sheepish. "Sorry, Jason. You're right."

"Actually," Proto said, "our caterers are not felons. I was able to match King Kong and Pinky to misdemeanors."

"I don't think that makes it any better, Proto," Jason said. "What did these two do?"

Proto flashed up a projection of two criminal records side by side. There were Pinky and King Kong, looking slightly younger, with glazed expressions on their faces. "They were arrested for breaking and entering five years ago. Disposition: $1,500 fine."

"No jail time," Maya read. "Just fined. Todd Wainright and Samantha Dooley. Look, their address in Los Angeles is the same."

Proto flashed up an image of a high-rise building. "The address appears to be associated with a university dormitory at the Los Angeles Institute of Technology. I wonder what they broke into."

"Hey," Jason said, "LAIT is the school where my mom taught before she joined Recode."

Proto flashed up an article from *The Sunset Tech*, LAIT's college newspaper. "It appears Mr. Wainright and Miss Dooley were university students when they broke into the school's prestigious computer science lab to prank one of their professors. Mr. Wainright was also on the wrestling team, and Samantha Dooley was president of the Electrical Engineering and Computing Club. Mr. Wainright served as vice president of the club during that time."

Maya stared at Jason. "Are you thinking what I'm thinking?"

"My mom is with a couple of fake caterers who all went to the same nerdy school?"

"No," Maya said. "Pinky and King Kong don't work for Recode, but they managed to pretend they're innocent caterers for the field trip. They have a fancy education at a leading academic institution in *technology—not* baking—and a pretty clean record. Then they show up here mysteriously and drive off with your mother. Are you getting it now?"

Jason's head was starting to hurt. "Will you just tell me, Maya? You're freaking me out."

"It means, Jason, that they are *good* at being *bad*."

Jason's eyes bulged at the sound of that word. He could practically hear his mother's voice ringing in his ear: "*You know, bad guys, Jason.*"

Proto seemed to be thinking the same thing. He took on an orange color. "Dr. Pascal often talks of people who seek to benefit themselves at the expense of others. Where there is good—"

"—there is evil," Jason finished.

BREAKING AND ENTERING

Jason sat on the family room couch. Maya sat beside him as Proto leapt to the arm of the sofa and took up post beside Jason.

"Look, we could be jumping to conclusions here," Jason said. "What if Wainright and Dooley are real Recode security employees, but undercover . . . to protect Mom or something? In the movies, companies hire ex-thieves to improve their security all the time. That's a possibility, right?"

Maya looked like she was thinking about it. "I suppose that could be true."

"Excellent theory, Jason," Proto said.

Jason got out his phone. "I want to try Mom again."

"Good idea," Maya said. "It can't hurt to call her to feel out the situation. Just don't say anything that would let people know you think something could be wrong. If she *is* with some bad guys, they're probably watching her every move."

"I'll send a normal text then." Jason thought up a message. "Something she'd normally respond to."

Can't wait for Aunty Dotty to come, even though your cooking is sooo much better.

Maya and Jason stared at the phone. After a minute went by, there was still no reply.

"Ugh," Jason said, frustrated. "I need to call Dad again. I have to. This doesn't feel right."

His father picked up. "What is it, Jase? I'm in the middle of a sale."

"Dad, I think . . ." Jason paused, unsure how to say it. "I think . . . you know that van I was talking about? It's not, it wasn't . . ." He frowned, knowing he was messing this up. "The people who drove Mom were caterers but not really— they're, they're criminal-slash-former-college students, who wrestled and ran a computer club." *Oh, man.* This was not coming out like it should. "I think something's wrong—"

"Jase," Ray Pascal said. "Have you been eating too many Pop-Tarts while Mom is out of town? I'm sure she's on her flight now. I'm swamped. I'll call you back later." He hung up.

Jason felt numb. He tossed his phone onto the coffee table. "Now what? This is insane." He pressed his hands to his forehead and thought about the van that took his mother away. "I know." He sat up. "Run the plates, Proto."

"Run the plates?" Proto repeated, his light blinking. "I'm not sure what is meant by this grammatically incorrect sentence. Did you mean you would like me to run *across* some plates?"

Jason let out a long breath. "Maya, you explain."

"Gladly," Maya said. "What he means is, access the Department of Motor Vehicles license plate registrations to see if we can identify the owner of the van. If it's Recode's van, then maybe Jason's theory is right, and these guys could be undercover security detail for Dr. Pascal or something. And read up on idioms, please. They're just as fascinating as French."

"*Absolument!*" Proto blinked momentarily. "Done and done. I've run the plates! The registered owner is a company: Al's New and Used Trucks. Purchased two months ago from Ford Motor Company. Now how do you like them apples?"

From his post on the arm of the sofa, Proto projected an image of a scruffy-looking truck lot on the edge of sprawling woods. There was a chain-link perimeter fence, numerous vehicles sitting on the paved lot, and a small one-story office.

Jason's stomach sank. "Al's New and Used Trucks?"

"I bet that means Pinky and King Kong stole the thing off the lot," Maya said.

"We have to go to the truck lot," Jason said.

"Maybe someone knows something there," Maya said. "Maybe Al's Trucks doesn't even know a vehicle was stolen yet. If they have security cameras, Pinky and King Kong could be caught on video. Then we'll have something for the police if they really did steal that van."

"Then the police will do something," Jason added.

"It is a well-conceived plan, Maya," Proto concurred. "I rather enjoy working on such interesting problems! Now we'll get to the bottom of this and crack this puppy wide open."

"You did read up on your idioms," Maya observed.

"Don't get too excited, Proto." Jason got to his feet. "This could be dangerous. Who's to say the people at the truck company aren't bad, too?"

"That's true," Maya said. "We'll need to armor up. I bet my DronePro could come in handy for something." She went to her backpack.

49

"Wait a second," Jason said. "You're coming with me?"

Maya stared at Jason. "Why wouldn't I come?"

"You're not the least bit afraid?"

Maya shouldered her backpack. "No, are you?"

Jason swallowed. "No."

"Actually," Proto interrupted, "I detect—"

"All right, all right, I'm nervous!" Jason admitted.

"I am, too," Maya said. "But it will be okay. You can't forget, we have the best armor around to protect *us* and your mom."

"We do?"

Maya gestured toward Proto. "We have Proto! Right?"

Jason started at the tiny spider-bot looking up at them from the arm of the sofa. "*Him?*"

"Me?" Proto said. "The best armor around?" His glow turned pink. "How I love such praise. I do not exactly know how I can protect you yet, but I will find out!"

Great, Jason thought. They were about to check out an old truck lot that could be filled with bad-guy types, and all they had for protection was an amateur AI and a DronePro. He went to the hall closet and grabbed his mom's old tennis racquet. It wasn't any better, but at least it was something. He stuck it in his backpack.

▷ ◁

With Proto's help, Jason and Maya covered the seven miles in thirty-seven minutes on their bikes. Dusty and winded, they slowed to a stop directly across the street from Al's Trucks.

Jason wiped sweat from his brow. He studied the shabby office and the big fenced-in lot beside it. The lot was full of new and used trucks and vans, but the office looked empty. No cars were parked in the customer lot.

"Terrific," Jason said. "The place is closed."

"You are correct, Jason," Proto piped up from his wrist. "Store Hours: Monday through Friday, 10 a.m. to 8 p.m. Closed Saturday and Sunday."

"It would have been helpful to know that *before* we left, Proto," Maya said. "Now what?"

Wait a second. Jason spotted an eyeball camera hanging from the eaves of the office. "Security cameras. Just like you thought, Maya. Proto, do you have a way to access the video those cameras record?"

"That's a negative, Jason," Proto said. "The security cameras are secure, meaning I would have to break the encryption to access the video, a certain violation of cybersecurity laws."

"There has to be another way," Maya said. "Let's move back into the trees. That camera could be recording us, for all we know."

They tucked their bikes within the tree line facing one side of the building and hid within the foliage. Maya reached into her backpack and pulled out her DronePro, which was about the size of a toy helicopter, except it looked way cooler. "I call her Patty, named after my great grandmother who was one of the first female pilots during World War II."

Proto turned bright blue. "What an intriguing device!"

Maya set it on the ground. As she dug in her backpack for the controller, Proto leaped off Jason's wrist and scrambled up to Patty. He studied her closely. "U.S. Patent #252562. Manufactured last year. Made in China. I will try to speak her language. *Nǐ hǎo ma. Wǒ jiào* Proto."

"Proto," Jason said, "Patty doesn't talk. She's just a machine."

"Oh." Proto's glow dimmed. "What a shame. Patty looks like she has such impressive features."

Maya pulled out the controller. "Check it out, Proto."

Patty's propellers began to spin, then she flew into the sky overhead.

Proto's glow became even brighter. "Patty is amazing! I am not designed to fly yet, but Dr. Pascal said that would be a future enhancement. I can't wait. Imagine what I could do from up there!"

Maya flew the DronePro around the perimeter of the truck lot while she used her phone to watch the video it was recording. "There must be a way to check out the building without being noticed." Maya maneuvered Patty to the back of the office building. "There! Since the rear of the building faces the forest, there aren't any cameras in back, so all we have to do is climb the fence to get closer."

"One moment," Proto said. "That is against statute 497c3 of our county laws. Trespassing on private property. I cannot violate the law."

Jason rolled his eyes. "Yes, you can, Proto; you already have. I'm pretty certain when you left the Recode Global building as a billion-dollar tech device, you broke a few rules."

"No, I did not," Proto said. "It was *you* who carried me out of the building."

"In that case . . ." Jason held out his wrist. "Shall we?"

Proto's glow dimmed as he climbed on. "I still do not approve."

Leaving their bikes behind, Maya and Jason slung on their backpacks and hurried to the fence. They climbed over quickly and quietly. Seconds later, they were squatting next to the building's back door.

Jason gently wiggled the door handle, but it was locked. "Now we just need to get in."

"Excuse me again," Proto whispered, sounding more annoyed. "Do you both intend to break in?"

"Maybe," Maya murmured.

"I feel I must warn you of an ethics theory called *consequentialism*, in which the morality of an act is decided by its consequences. The issue is often connected with phrases such as, 'Who are you to play God?'"

Jason looked at Maya, who shrugged. Proto definitely sounded like his mom talking.

"Listen, Proto," Jason whispered. "We're not going to hurt anybody, break anything, or wreck this business's future. We're only going to sneak in, see if we can pull up some security video, and find any info that could help my mom. If we find something, we'll tip off the police. It's a little bit of not-really-that-bad to accomplish something really, really good."

"But I feel I must keep you from sliding down what is referred to as 'a slippery slope' toward worse criminal activity."

Jason sighed. "Does that mean you won't scour the Internet to figure out how to pick the door lock for us?"

"I will not."

Jason pulled out his phone. "Then I will."

"I do not recommend this," Proto warned.

As Jason and Proto bickered, Maya examined a dead plant in a small flower pot beside the back door. She lifted the pot and held up a brass key.

"Al's Trucks isn't exactly a fortress," Maya whispered.

"Terrific," Jason said quietly. "Slippery slope avoided, Proto. Is it still breaking in if we have the key?"

SEVEN SOLDIERS OF DOOM

Jason inserted the key into the lock before Proto could debate the point. Once inside, Jason and Maya used their phones to light up a dark office space. The window shades to the front of the building were drawn, and the place looked to be from an older time period—an older, messier one. Jason and Maya wandered around a large room with a dusty water cooler, a couple of rickety wooden desks, old-fashioned landline phones, and a tiny, gross bathroom and closet off to the side.

Jason's heart pounded with nervousness. "We better hurry. This won't look good if someone walks in on us. Proto, alert us if you sense any people or cars coming near the building while we search the place."

"Very well, Jason," Proto muttered, still clearly perturbed.

Jason walked around the room, looking for video monitoring screens. "Not a single computer?" He groaned. "How is that even possible?" Instead there were files and papers stacked on the desk surfaces, several chairs, and the floor. There were also two rusty metal file cabinets as holey as Swiss cheese.

"Maybe the cameras' video recordings are monitored remotely," Maya whispered. "Those cameras outside could be connected to the cloud instead of a physical hard drive."

"Oh, great!" Jason said. "You mean this ratty old place has fancy security cameras?" *They had broken in for nothing?*

Maya looked around the room. "Maybe there's something else here that could connect King Kong and Pinky to this place."

"I'll check out the closet," Jason said.

"Wait," Maya said. "Look!" She pointed at a yellowed picture tacked to the wall beside the bathroom. She moved in closer. "Al's Trucks: Little League Championship. Isn't that a younger version of King Kong on this team?"

Jason joined Maya by the photo. No one could miss the six-foot-tall twelve-year-old, standing in the back row of a baseball team. "I bet that older guy wearing the Al's Trucks T-shirt is Al, King Kong's father. They look so much alike."

This was getting fishier by the minute. Jason swallowed as he thought about his mother. *Taken.*

Suddenly, there came a thump against the back door.

"What was that?" Maya asked.

"I believe it was some sort of canine," Proto said. "Or perhaps a lagomorph."

"A lago-what?" Maya said.

"More specifically, a rabbit."

Next Jason heard claws scrape against wood, then a muffled series of barks. "That's no rabbit. We gotta go." He pulled his tennis racket from his backpack. "This place has guard dogs."

"Guard dogs?" Maya groaned. "Why didn't you say anything before, Proto?"

"You requested I monitor persons and vehicles. You said nothing about dogs."

"Oh man," Jason groaned. *Why did Proto have to be so literal all the time?*

There was another thump at the storefront windows. Jason and Maya whipped their heads in the direction of the sound.

A tiny dog with pointy ears was silhouetted behind the drawn shade. Jason let out a sigh of relief.

"It looks like a Chihuahua," Maya said. "How cute!"

"A quick web search reveals Chihuahuas are praised for their protective nature as guard dogs," Proto said, "not only for their ferocity, but also their ability to draw attention to suspicious activity by barking."

"That little guy? Ferocious?" Maya said. "Maybe we should let the doggie in. Let's put him in the bathroom until we're done searching the place."

The dog disappeared again, and more muffled barks came from the back.

"Persistent pooch," Jason said, returning his racquet to his backpack. He hurried toward the back door to let the dog in. He cracked open the door, just to be safe, and sure enough, a cute little black-and-white spotted Chihuahua was staring up at him, wagging his tail. "Hey, little guy."

"Actually, Jason," Proto said. "There's something I must tell you."

"Not now, Proto," Jason said, "You could scare the thing, and he could start barking again." Jason did his best to sound disarming. "Come in, puppy, puppy!"

He opened the door wider, and the Chihuahua rushed in, but the dog's demeanor went from innocent to murderous in less than a second. Then six more Chihuahuas of various colors blew in, barking their heads off, practically knocking Jason over. "What the . . ."

"That was what I wanted to warn you about," Proto said.

Jason groped for his tennis racquet on his back as four of the dogs darted toward Maya.

Maya leapt onto one of the desks and screamed. The dogs circled Maya's desk, snarling and leaping in vain as Jason danced around with his own attackers.

A spotted Chihuahua had a grip on Jason's sock. Jason tried to loosen the pup's hold with the edge of his tennis racket.

"Don't kill him," Maya squealed. "He's still a tiny dog!"

"I'm more worried about me than them," Jason said. A second dog had a firm grip on the tongue of his sneaker, and then a third bounded from the floor and nipped Jason's calf. "Ow!"

"This is causing a worrisome level of noise," Proto said.

"Would you help me, Proto?" Jason yelled. "These. Things. Hurt!"

"What can I do?" Proto asked.

"Distract them!" Jason yelled.

"Ah," Proto said. "I know!"

Beams of light streamed from Proto's watch-like face. Images of tiny sweaters, booties, and blingy collars danced along the linoleum.

The dogs suddenly stopped to stare at the images.

"My research indicates Chihuahuas have incredible fashion sense."

"It's working," Jason said. "We gotta get out of here." He headed for the back door. But as soon as Maya jumped off the desk with a thud, the dogs snapped back to attention and started barking again.

"Run!" Proto ordered.

Maya managed to get out first with Jason close behind, followed by seven soldiers of doom. As Jason ascended the fence, a trio of Chihuahuas latched onto his sneakers. Maya was doing slightly better. Only one Chihuahua was holding fiercely onto her backpack, while three were bouncing around below. "More distractions, Proto!" Maya shouted.

Suddenly, the air all around them was filled with ghost-like images of running squirrels, bouncing tennis balls, steaks on skateboards, and more. The skateboards worked! Seven Chihuahuas swiftly flew into the air to lunge after their new rolling holo-prey.

At last, Jason and Maya made it over the fence. A chorus of dog barks faded away behind them. They ran toward their bikes hidden in the woods.

"Next time, Proto," Jason said, "watch for *everything* unusual."

"Roger that," Proto said. "We make a good team, don't we?"

Jason sat on his bed and tended to his wounds while Maya inspected her backpack at Jason's desk. Jason's ankles were dog-ravaged pincushions, smarting every time he applied antiseptic at a bloody nip, but Maya's legs were remarkably free of marks. Her backpack had seen better days though. "Nothing a few more patches can't fix," Maya said. She inspected the interior of her bag. "At least Patty is okay."

"Excellent news," Proto said. He stood on the surface of Jason's desk. "It would be terrible if anything happened to such a fine machine."

"I can't believe I got shredded by Chihuahuas for nothing," Jason moped.

Maya gave him a sympathetic look. "Sorry about what happened, Jason. Maybe your dad is right, and Pinky and King Kong are just escorting your mother to the airport. We could have blown this whole thing out of proportion."

"But how do you explain the suspicious van logo thing?"

"Well . . ." Maya looked uncertain. "Maybe King Kong just borrowed one of his dad's vans for the security detail job, and that's it. It could be as simple as that, right?"

Jason collapsed backward onto his bed. "Maybe," he said. He pulled his phone from his pocket. "Still nothing from Mom."

Suddenly, the sound of pop music emanated from Maya's backpack. "That's *my* mother."

She pulled her phone out of one of the pockets and looked at the screen. "Oh man, I can't believe it's already four! I'll let her go to voicemail." She started texting instead. "On my way back," she muttered to herself as she punched in her message. "We have been working on . . . a science project. So sorry."

"Science project?" Proto asked. "Is that what we have been doing, Maya?"

"Uh, I wouldn't call it that," Maya said.

"But you just did," Proto said. His glow began to blink as though confused.

Jason and Maya looked at each other.

"I'll take this one," Jason said. "Proto, one day you will learn that sometimes, you have to bend the truth for the greater good."

"Bend the truth," Proto repeated. "*Merriam-Webster's* definition: 'To say something that is not completely true to achieve a goal.' Does that mean if Maya had told her mother she had been busy searching a truck sales office in the middle of the afternoon with you, and then was detained because she was chased by seven Chihuahuas, a goal would not be achieved?"

"Yes," Jason said. "That is correct."

"And what is that goal?"

"To stay out of trouble with my mom," Maya answered.

"I see!" Proto said. "Bending the truth fits in nicely with consequentialism then. You were weighing the consequences of telling the complete truth with bending the truth. I will have to try this sometime!"

Jason turned onto his stomach and groaned into his pillow. "Great. I think I just taught Proto how to lie. Mom's going to *love* that one, *if* I ever see her again."

Maya put her phone away and stared at Jason. "Listen, I better go, Jason."

Jason didn't move.

"If you need me, just text." Maya got up to leave, but then she stopped herself. She retrieved the DronePro from her bag. "I'll leave Patty here. I know how much you like her. Keep her for as long as you want."

Jason sighed. "Thanks, Maya," he said. "I'm sure things are perfectly fine," even though he felt they were anything but.

After Maya left, Jason rolled onto his side.

Proto climbed onto Jason's chest. "Jason? Are you unwell?"

"Sorry, Proto," Jason said. "I just need some space, I think."

Proto backed up a few inches. "Is this enough?"

Jason groaned again.

Soon after, a door slammed downstairs. "I'm home!"

Ray Pascal said. "Jase, you're going to have to clean all the dirt you tracked into the house, you know!"

Jason didn't respond.

"Jason?" his dad called up the stairs.

"Coming, Dad!" Jason yelled.

His father began to whistle a cheerful tune and the sound faded away into another part of the house. Jason heaved himself off his bed and started down the stairs. "Proto, I can't stand this," he whispered. "It's too much for me. I have to tell Dad so he gets what is really going on."

Before Proto could respond, the doorbell rang.

That's weird. Jason paused on the stairs. *Hardly anyone ever rings the doorbell.* He debated answering the door.

Then he heard his father undoing the deadbolt and opening it himself. "Can I help you?" his father said.

A male voice answered. "Good evening, Mr. Pascal. I'm Dr. Leo Cooper from Recode Global. We've met before."

"Oh, yes, I remember. Hi."

"Hello, Mr. Pascal," a second, deeper voice added. "I'm Agent Sparks with the FBI."

A DEADLY DEADLINE

Several miles away, a man entered a dark office and removed his baseball cap. He ran a hand through his salt-and-pepper hair, then sank into a deep leather chair situated behind his desk.

"Illuminate," he said.

Bright lights shone from the ceiling. "Welcome back, Thaddeus," said a pleasant female voice that filled the room. Thaddeus's desk was a massive thing. It was once his father's. It had four claw-footed legs with segments resembling the joint connections of a large beast's legs and shoulders. One end had a metal lion skull, complete with pointed teeth that jutted out; the skull's level top served as a resting place for an empty coffee cup.

The rest of the office was minimalist: no file cabinets or other furniture, and no visible computer. Flat panels covered the front, left, and right walls. When the lights activated, so did the left and front screens. They displayed a complex algebraic equation.

"Solve for x, Thaddeus," the voice said.

The man examined the screens as he performed calculations in his head. "Nina, x equals 13.147."

"That is correct," Nina, the bodyless voice, said. "Completed with twenty seconds to spare." Applause rang throughout the room.

"Nothing like a little math to relax the mind," Thaddeus remarked.

"Is something troubling you?"

Before Thaddeus could answer, a louder female voice boomed into the room. "THADDEUSSSSS!"

Thaddeus swallowed. His most demanding client always had a way of making a surprise auditory entrance into his office. He wondered what it would be this time.

A life-sized avatar formed in front of him. She was a five-foot-four virtual representation of his client who called herself Madame X. She was an *x* of a problem that Thaddeus just could not solve or get rid of. He had never seen or spoken to the person or even the "it" behind her avatar, and for all Thaddeus knew, Madame X was an extraterrestrial, or a super-genius elder-baby, or a mutant earthworm on growth hormones.

When Madame finished taking shape, she was cloaked to the floor. Her eyes emitted a mesmerizing light within the darkness of the hood of her robe. Then she pushed back her hood and unveiled the face of a Burmese python with a flicking forked tongue.

Thaddeus held back a wince.

"*Jusssssst* wanted to check in on our little project," Madame said at a more reasonable volume, though her voice was not nearly as pleasant as Nina's.

"We have secured Dr. Pascal," Thaddeus said. "She is here, safe and sound, and has already started work on the second prototype." Thaddeus tapped a different section of the desk, activating a panel behind him that connected to cameras in the safe room where Dr. Pascal was secured.

Dr. Pascal was seated at a wide, U-shaped table. She seemed unaware of the camera as she worked. The table was littered with all sorts of parts, tools, and wires as if an electronics store had been raided for all of its contents. The walls of her room were lined with racks of assorted equipment with dials, LED displays, and flashing lights

"This is wonderful," Madame X said. "I trust you have been keeping your team on a need-to-know basis regarding Dr. Pascal's kidnapping."

Thaddeus nodded. "Aside from us, Dooley, and Wainright, no one knows. Recode Global and her family think she is headed for a conference in Switzerland."

"Good," Madame said. "That should keep everyone in the dark while we carry on with our plans. I imagine they will ssssoon catch on that Dr. Pascal is missing, but . . ." Madame swiveled her serpent head in Thaddeus's direction. ". . . the authoritiessss are no match for me. Are they?"

"No, Madame," Thaddeus replied.

Madame X returned to studying Dr. Pascal on the monitor. "I see she has everything she needs."

"Yes, everything," *Except Proto*, Thaddeus thought, but he wouldn't mention that to Madame. Instead, he had his cohorts make a similar non-operational replica, which was given to Dr. Pascal to use as a model for her project.

"I can hardly wait until we bring our new prototype online," Madame X said. "I've already thought of a name for it—do you want to guess what that name could be?"

Madame didn't even wait for Thaddeus to respond. "*Monsieur Y!* Isn't that sssstupendous?"

"Sounds like you've found the perfect match," Thaddeus said.

"Indeed," Madame X said. "Before you know it, we'll have Monsieur Y work with me to create a perfect Z, then we'll have to sssstart all over with the alphabet as our army of AI, programmed with *my* heurissstics, is in place." Madame paused, then her voice turned into one of concern. "Has Dr. Pascal had anything to eat?"

"Er, not yet," Thaddeus said, lamenting in his mind his failed plans to steal Proto. His team had executed their plan almost flawlessly. They had figured out how to bring down Recode Global's electrical system to generate a distraction and get past the security measures to enter Dr. Pascal's lab, only to discover that Proto was gone. "I figured we could order something to eat for Dr. Pascal later."

"Make sure she is well nourished," Madame X said, "ssssso she's comfortable. Understand?"

"Yes, Madame," Thaddeus said.

She slithered in closer until her jaws were only a fang's distance from his face. "Thaddeus, how long have you been working with me?"

"About ten years." But it seemed much, much longer.

"And you are pleasssed with your time in my employ?"

"Exceptionally." *Not.* Even though Thaddeus made a considerable amount of money working for Madame, the constant worry over unexpectedly dying at Madame's whim had been a bit of a downer.

Madame's snake-like head wavered in front of him. "You know, I still misssssss dear Reginald."

Thaddeus did his best to keep his composure, though the memory of his father and former business partner still felt fresh. Reginald refused to accept Madame as a client of his company, which was once a respected top-rated cybersecurity company. Then less than twenty-four hours after he declined Madame's business, Reginald disappeared. In his place, Thaddeus received a special delivery from FedEx, containing Reginald's cane and a thank-you note that read: *The future is ours to build. I am looking forward to our partnership, Thaddeus. Respectfully, Madame X.*

"Your father would have been impressed to know we are *this* close to ussssurping Recode's power over us." Madame's serpent-head backed off, giving Thaddeus some room to breathe. She covered her head with the hood of her robe again. "Notice the world out there. A disaster. I can hardly look at it." Her glowing eyes dimmed. "Did you know my childhood was spent in poverty, in a perpetual state of want? I had to face unspeakable atrocities, fight for every piece of bread, every sip of water, and after all this time, it is still like that today for millions! The world cannot be allowed to stay this way. Society might rise above such folly."

The avatar began to shrink in her robe like the Wicked Witch in *The Wizard of Oz.* "Technology is the answer, but it hasn't been able to change the dismal mentality and tragically selfish behavior of humankind."

Thaddeus watched Madame X's empty robe puddle to the floor.

"Then I thought," Madame continued, "if I can make the universe a better place, than why not?"

Madame's robe changed into a crumpled white and silver ballgown. Then the dress rose from the floor as a beautiful woman's hands, then arms, came out of the sleeves, and a woman's head and neck ascended from the collar. Madame's avatar had long blond hair, which appeared as strands of gold. Her lips were cherry red. "Why squander my gifts like that?" She placed a manicured hand on her hip as her dress swished from the question.

Thaddeus had never seen Madame appear so beautiful. Was this what she looked like when she was in a good mood? "Uh, I don't know?"

"Exactly! There *is* no reason! Better, instead, to start over. Would you agree?"

Thaddeus nodded with forced eagerness.

"We have a specific timetable," Madame X continued. "Six days until Earth arrives at the ideal location for a new beginning."

What beginning? Thaddeus thought. "Six days?" he asked. "Why?"

"Too many questions," Madame X replied. "Please have the prototype ready in three."

Three days? Was that it? That meant Dr. Pascal would have to have a working prototype done tomorrow, so that Dooley and Wainright still had time to program the AI according to Madame's liking. Could Dr. Pascal finish months of work that fast? He thought of Proto again. If he just had Proto, it would make everyone's lives easier.

"We will get it done," he said confidently.

Madame smiled, then a wand materialized in her hand. She swooshed it in a circle. Glitter trailed through the air. "Carry on then, Thaddeus."

She dissolved into thin air.

Thaddeus let out a long breath. "Nina, give me another math problem."

"Would you like one that is easier or harder than the last one?" Nina said pleasantly.

"Harder."

"Certainly."

As Thaddeus worked out the equation, he ruminated about his larger problem in the back of his mind. He already had his team on the inside trying to track Proto, but Proto's internal security protocols were more advanced than they had anticipated.

Thaddeus never liked deadlines, but Madame X's deadlines were not ones he could miss.

Her deadlines actually meant *death*.

IF YOU NOTICE ANYTHING FUNNY

Jason swallowed. The FBI? He quietly backed up the stairs. "What's this about?" Jason's dad asked.

"Why don't we have a seat, sir?" the agent said.

"Sure," Mr. Pascal replied. "Of course."

Jason heard their footsteps fade away. Dad must have taken them to the living room.

"Proto," Jason whispered, "I have to know what's going on. Can you still hear them?"

"Yes," Proto whispered back. "I'll amplify it for you."

Immediately their voices came into Jason's ear. "Mr. Pascal," Dr. Cooper said, "it seems we experienced some electrical disturbances at Recode Global during Dr. Pascal's presentation."

Jason had to get a good look at these guys. What if they weren't who they said they were, like the Cupcake caterers? "Proto, is there any way you can *see* them?"

"I must have a visual line of sight to observe their physical features," Proto said.

"Quick then, disguise yourself."

Proto wrapped himself around Jason's wrist and presented himself as a Timex.

Just as Jason was about to bound down the steps and pretend like he was clueless about everything, he stopped himself. What if these guys weren't here to talk to his dad about his mom but were looking for *Proto*? Dr. Cooper, Mom's boss, would surely recognize him, even as a sports watch.

He tiptoed back to his room just as the FBI agent began questioning his father. "When was the last time you saw Dr. Pascal?"

"What's wrong, Jason?" Proto said in Jason's ear.

"They can't see you," Jason whispered. "Mom said there were bad guys. What if Dr. Cooper or the agent are up to no good? You need better cover."

Back in his room, Jason tried to think about how to get Proto in the living room with a clear line of sight without being noticed. He spotted the DronePro on his desk. "I've got an idea. Blend in with Patty."

Proto glowed. "Excellent idea, Jason." He climbed on top of Patty and made himself look just like another propeller. "How do you like me now?"

"Terrific. Now watch and record *everything*, Proto."

"You can depend on me," Proto said.

Minutes later, Jason hurried down the stairs while carrying the DronePro as casually as he could. As he headed toward the living room, he called out to his father. "Hey Dad, I'm taking Maya's DronePro out for a spin." He rounded the corner. His father was hunched over on the sofa. His forehead was creased, and his mouth was a tight line. Two men sat in the armchairs across from his dad. Jason recognized one of them as Dr. Cooper, the dude from Recode Global with the Albert Einstein hair, still in his lab coat. Sitting in the matching armchair was a skinny bald man in a navy suit, wearing a tightly hitched necktie. He appeared to be a standard-issue FBI agent, not that he'd ever met one before in real life.

Jason feigned surprise at the sight of them. "Oh, hi."

The agent stared at Jason with an intense gaze as if he was using X-ray vision to see into Jason's brain.

Jason started to sweat a little. His grip on the DronePro tightened.

"Jason," Ray said, clearing his throat, "why don't you give us a few minutes?"

"If you don't mind," the agent cut in, "your son should stay. Perhaps he could be helpful. Weren't you saying, Mr. Pascal, that Jason called you a number of times today about his mother?" He gestured toward the sofa. "Please, Jason, sit."

Mr. Pascal gave Jason a look to follow orders.

Jason took a seat beside his dad. He kept the DronePro in his lap.

"Hello, Jason." Dr. Cooper held out an outstretched hand over the coffee table.

Jason shook it, even though he didn't want to. Dr. Cooper was even sweatier than Jason felt. "I came with Agent Sparks."

Agent Sparks gave him a nod.

"I am not certain what I am watching for," Proto whispered in Jason's ear, "but I can say that everyone's heartbeats are elevated. Agent Sparks also appears to be physically distressed from something he has eaten earlier today, judging by the sounds from his stomach, and Dr. Cooper is showing slight traces of asthma in his breathing."

Jason tried not to react to Proto. He wished he had remembered to tell Proto not to talk.

"Tell me, Jason," Agent Sparks said, "what were you trying to say to your father about these, uh, casting directors and your mother?"

"Wait, what's this about?" Jason said.

"Your mother was supposed to meet me at the airport," Dr. Cooper said, "but she never showed."

Proto answered at the same time. "It appears they are investigating the whereabouts of your mother. They already said that when we were upstairs."

Jason swiped at his ear. "Wait, what did you say?" He wished he could tell Proto to shut it.

Dr. Cooper looked at him funny. "I said, your mother never showed at the airport."

This was not good. "Then where is she?" Jason managed.

"That's what we're trying to find out," Agent Sparks replied.

"I do not know, Jason," Proto said at the same time. "Perhaps these gentlemen can determine this."

Urgh.

"Now about those casting directors—" Sparks continued.

"Caterers," Jason corrected. Now that his father was aware that something was wrong, there was no way he could not talk about what he had seen. "I saw her with caterers at our house, the ones from Sugar-N-Spice, except they appeared in a Recode Global van. They drove her away."

Mr. Pascal stared at him, mouth open. "Why didn't you tell me that important detail, Jason?"

Jason stared at his father. "*I was trying to.*"

"Caterers in a Recode Global van?" Agent Sparks said, then he covered his mouth to stifle a burp. He turned to Dr. Cooper. "Does your company employ caterers for transportation purposes, too?"

Dr. Cooper looked annoyed by the question. "No, of course not."

Proto chose that moment to add information. "Dr. Cooper has hearing aids in both of his ears. They emit sound in frequency bands that are too high for human perception, but I find it mildly irritating."

Jason wanted to tell Proto that *he* was mildly irritating.

"The caterers *had* to have taken Mom," Jason emphasized.

Agent Sparks's face turned even more serious. He pulled a notepad and pen from the inside of his jacket. "What did they look like?"

Before Jason could speak, Proto immediately began describing King Kong and Pinky in his ear, except Proto's explanation was more detailed and included estimations of basal body temperature and descriptions of tiny tattoos on of the inside of Pinky's wrists. Jason could barely hear himself as he attempted to answer Agent Sparks's question.

"Excuse me, what did you say, Jason?" Agent Sparks said. "Rinky is at least seven feet tall and Ding Dong has a pink tattoo?"

"No, that's not what I meant."

Agent Sparks studied Jason up and down as though he were guilty of something. "Are you nervous, son?"

Jason's dad spoke up. "Watch your tone, Sparks. Clearly my son is upset about his mother, can't you tell? What kind of agent are you?"

"A good one," Sparks said coolly.

"Yes, I'm upset about my mom," Jason said. "And there's this . . . uh . . . *fly* buzzing around my ear, distracting me."

"Jason, are you trying to tell *me* something?" Proto asked.

Jason swatted at the pretend fly again. "I can't seem to stop it, but I wish it would quit buzzing."

"I think you *do* mean me," Proto whispered. "I will be quiet. Mum's the word."

Thank goodness. Jason started his answer over again and gave Agent Sparks a more accurate description of the fake caterers, minus the body temps.

Agent Sparks asked another question. "Recently, has your mother said or done anything out of the ordinary?"

Jason pretended to think the question over deeply, even though the image of his mother with Proto in her lab immediately flashed in his mind. "No."

"What about you, Mr. Pascal? Any strange behavior. Anything unusual?"

Ray's face looked strained. "Unusual? No . . . wait a second." He stiffened. "Are you trying to suggest something about my wife now?"

"Well," Dr. Cooper said, wringing his hands, "one of Dr. Pascal's highly classified and valuable projects is missing."

Oh no, Jason thought. They *do* think his mother stole Proto! Should he confess what he knew? He stared down at Proto, who was still doing a great impression of a DronePro propeller.

"This is ridiculous!" Ray Pascal snarled. "Leo, you've known Shannon for years. You *know* she'd never break a law, much less do anything to harm your company!"

Jason glanced at his distraught father.

No, no. Jason couldn't say anything. Where there was good, there was evil. Mom had warned him. It was more important to find her right now. Clearing her name could come later. *Proto must be kept secret,* even from Dad, to protect both of his parents.

"I completely agree with you, Ray," Dr. Cooper said, raising his hands in a calming gesture. "We are only discussing possibilities. She could very well be acting against her will or, perhaps, without her knowledge."

"These caterers," Agent Sparks said, "or whoever they may be, are very likely connected."

"No kidding, Sherlock," his father seethed.

Jason put a hand on his dad's back. It was hard to see him as upset as he was. "We know Mom didn't do anything, Dad. She's tough. She'll be okay." Jason didn't quite believe his own words, but it seemed like the right thing to say.

"Listen to your son," Dr. Cooper said. "Jason gave us a good lead to work with to help figure this out. We all want what's best for Shannon and her safety."

Ray nodded, then turned to his son. "I'm so sorry, Jase. I should have listened to you. I could have done something."

Agent Sparks returned his pen and his notepad to his jacket. "You still can, Mr. Pascal. I'd like you to come with us to answer more questions and verify a few other things. It could mean a great deal to our investigation. It should only take a few hours."

"Of course," Ray Pascal said, getting up.

Just then, the doorbell rang.

"Helloooooo!" Jason heard his aunt's voice calling at the front door. "I'm here to make someone's favorite spaghetti!"

"Perfect timing," Ray said. "That's my sister. Dr. Pascal arranged for her to come over to help us while she's . . ." His voice faded. ". . . gone."

Jason thought his dad might cry for a second. *Stay strong, Dad*, he thought.

"Remember," Agent Sparks said quickly, "this is still an open investigation. Carry on like nothing has happened. Same with you, Jason. Can you keep a secret?"

Jason nodded, holding the DronePro with a death grip now. He could keep a billion-dollar secret if he had to.

His dad looked toward the front door. "I'll just let Dotty know I have to take care of important paperwork at the shop."

"That's good." Agent Sparks glanced around the room. "Is there another way to exit? We can wait for you in our car."

Jason heard more knocking.

"Anyone home?" his aunt called.

"Jason," his father said, "show them out through the side door. I'll let Aunt Dotty in."

Jason did as he was told, carrying the DronePro under his arm. He walked Dr. Cooper and Agent Sparks through the kitchen and opened the door that led to the side yard.

Dr. Cooper stepped outside but before Agent Sparks made his exit, he turned to Jason. "Neat toy you've got there, son. I hear the DronePro is a brilliant gadget."

Jason swallowed the lump that had suddenly grown in his throat. "Yup, it's brilliant."

"We'll find your mother," Dr. Cooper added. "There's nothing to worry about."

Agent Sparks handed Jason a business card. "If you notice anything funny or think of anything else, you've got my number."

Jason took the card. "Thanks." Then he stepped back from the door as Agent Sparks dropped his gaze to the DronePro again.

"Nice meeting you!" Jason shut the door, glad to be rid of both of them.

"Jaaaaay-son!" Aunt Dotty called from somewhere inside the house. "Where are you?"

Jason returned to the living room. His aunt was rifling through plastic sacks of groceries in the foyer. Unlike his father, Jason's aunt wasn't all that big, but she made up for her petite size with a ton of spunk.

"Your dad just let me know he won't be joining us for dinner," Aunt Dotty said. "What a rush he was in." She placed her hands on her hips. "No bother, that just means more for us! Can you help me get everything into the kitchen?"

"Sure," Jason said, trying to act as though everything was normal. He set down the DronePro in the foyer and picked up a few bags. As he hauled them to the kitchen, he started pondering his next move.

He didn't know if he could trust Dr. Cooper. He pulled groceries out of bags and set them on the kitchen counter. Nor could he depend upon an FBI agent who couldn't spot a liar when he saw one. And his dad? He was too stressed out to be useful.

Jason pulled out tomatoes and fresh herbs from a bag and set them on the counter.

Like it or not, he'd have to lead the investigation himself.

"Excuse me, Jason," Proto said in his ear. "May I speak now?"

Jason stiffened, forgetting he had left Proto with Patty in the foyer. Then he noticed something dart from the living room into the kitchen out of the corner of his eye.

Aunt Dotty was putting groceries in the fridge.

"Don't move!" Jason said, but he didn't mean to say it quite that loudly.

Proto froze under the breakfast table.

"What's the matter, Jason?" Aunt Dotty asked.

"Uh, uh," Jason said. "I just saw a giant spider."

"I have been recording everything, Jason," Proto said. "And there is no spider in this room. However, we should discuss what just happened with the FBI agent and Dr. Cooper."

Jason groaned. Why was Proto always chiming in at the worst possible moments?

"Is it that big?" Aunt Dotty began to look all around the room. "Where is it?"

"It just went that way." Jason pointed in the opposite direction where Proto was.

Aunt Dotty flew into action. "I'll get it."

As she searched the kitchen for something to catch the spider with, Jason grabbed Proto from the floor and hid him in his pocket. "Listen, Aunt Dotty, I have a huge science project due tomorrow. Is it okay if my partner Maya comes over tonight so we can finish it up?"

"Bending the truth again," Proto said in his ear, cheerfully. "You are very good at this."

Jason ignored Proto just as Aunt Dotty turned with a paper towel in her hand. "Go on, Jason," she said. "Don't you worry. Tell Maya there will be plenty of spaghetti for her, too. Now go on upstairs. I'll find the bug and set him free. It's bad luck to kill a spider, you know."

Jason let out a sigh of relief over the close call of Proto nearly being spotted. He ascended the stairs and whispered to Proto, "We have got to work on your lo-lo-whatever you call it."

"Loquacity?" Proto finished.

"Yeah, that. And you almost got spotted."

"I assure you, Aunt Dotty would not have seen me," Proto said, climbing out of Jason's pocket and clamping on to Jason's wrist. "I calculated the range of her peripheral vision between the counter and the refrigerator as well as her intended direction of travel based on the position of her body and her gait speed. I was far out of her visual range."

"She still could have seen you."

Proto glowed orange. "Could not."

"You're probably right," Jason said as he entered the room. "But let me put it this way, Proto." He shut the door. "No one but me and Maya know I have you. I'd like to keep it that way. Now let's call Maya. We've got important work to do."

"I believe you are referencing your science project. Is that correct?"

"Exactly."

"That is terrific, Jason," Proto said, glowing a happy blue. "I will be of significant use as I am extremely knowledge-able about this field of study!"

"I'm sure you are."

Jason pulled his phone from his pocket and made the call to Maya.

SPEAK OF THE DEVIL

Thaddeus paced back and forth in his office. He'd been watching Dr. Pascal work for hours, all the while hoping Dooley and Wainright were getting closer to locating Proto. It wouldn't be long before Madame X realized he was stalling. Thaddeus sat back down again, then nearly fell out of his chair when he saw the huge white tiger lying on his desk, licking a paw. *Speak of the devil.*

"Helloooo, Thaddeus," the tiger said in Madame X's voice. "Sorry to bother you so soon, but this project of ours is much too important to neglect. How is Dr. Pascal's progress?"

"F-f-f-fine," Thaddeus stuttered. Madame's virtual cat breath was nauseating him. He rolled his chair back a couple of inches. "She is almost done with the mechanical design of the physical device."

The tiger's tail thumped against the desk with pleasure. "Puuurrrfect."

"Would you like to speak with her now, Madame?" Thaddeus asked.

"No . . ." Madame sniffed the air. "I prefer to keep a low profile. Lie in the grass, if you will."

"As you wish," Thaddeus said. "Dr. Pascal is about to begin the most challenging and tricky parts of the proto- type's design. It could take her some time."

"Of course," the tiger said. "She's talented, but only human."

The tiger yawned.

Thaddeus tried not to stare at Madame's razor-sharp teeth.

"And she's eaten?" Madame continued.

"Not yet," Thaddeus answered. "She's requested a num- ber of takeout menus. I imagine she'll choose something eventually."

"Very well." Madame licked her lips. "Intelligence needs nourishment, after all. Speaking of which, all this talk about food is making *me* hungry."

A giant bloody carcass of an unidentifiable animal sud- denly appeared on Thaddeus's desk. Madame pounced on top of it, snarling.

Thaddeus recoiled in disgust as Madame clawed the sinewy muscles of her dead prey and then ripped into the flesh with her teeth. With blood dripping from her massive jaws, she turned and gave Thaddeus a slight grin.

Thaddeus tried to keep a straight face. He despised Madame, but she could *never* know that.

Finally, Madame swallowed, then licked her lips. "When is Dr. Pascal projecting completion?"

"Possibly as soon as . . . as tomorrow," Thaddeus lied, "then we'll begin deploying our code as planned." Even though he knew it was impossible to build a working prototype that fast without Proto, Thaddeus had no choice but to deceive Madame.

"I'm looking forward to tomorrow then." Madame's tail waived in the air with pleasure.

"Yes, Wainright just let me know they are hard at work building the convolutional neural network," Thaddeus said, "based upon the design parameters you submitted." *Not.* The last he had heard they were still trying to hack into Proto's security parameters to identify its location.

"Good, Thaddeus," Madame X purred. "You never let me down."

Thaddeus nodded. He stared at his father's desk. He *couldn't* let Madame X down.

Madame then swiped the leftover carcass off the desk. "The Siberian tiger has no predators, Thaddeus. Did you know this?"

"Yes, Madame." Thaddeus hoped he had answered correctly.

"The tiger decides who lives and who dies. Are you following me, Thaddeus?"

"Very much so, Madame." Thaddeus was certain he knew his fate if he didn't find Proto soon. At the rate they were going, it would take them months to finish a replica of Proto.

Madame leapt onto the floor and began to circle Thaddeus's desk. "Together, we will leave this rotting, good-for-nothing cesspool of a society," she said, seething. "Earth has become a primitive jungle in which we no longer can live!" She paused in front of the desk, then stood on her hind legs. She dropped her heavy front paws on the edge of Thaddeus's desk. "We must head for the stars!"

"The stars, Madame?" Thaddeus dared to ask. "Does this have something to do with that six days you were talking about? Are we going somewhere?"

"Yes, yes, Thaddeus. You are quick to catch on. I believe it is time you knew some of my plans. You have proven your worth by obtaining Dr. Pascal and Proto." Madame's tiger body then morphed into a spitting image of Darth Vader. She inhaled and exhaled deeply, making Darth Vader's horrible signature breathing sound. *Inhale. Exhale. Inhale.* "I have built us a starship, my son, and identified all the other worthy individuals who will come with us." *Exhale.*

Thaddeus tried not to flinch at the label "son." He knew exactly who his father had been, and Darth Vader/Madame X was not even close.

"My brilliance sometimes even surprises me, Thaddeus." *Inhale.* "I have concluded we can locate a habitable planet outside of our solar system with 85.7 percent probability of success."

Eighty-five point seven percent? Thaddeus wondered. What were the chances they could survive a journey that far? And what if they weren't successful in finding another habitable planet?

"I can tell what you are thinking," Madame X said between raspy breaths. "There is no need to worry. Our chances go up as soon as we have Monsieur Y, guided by our objectives, to aid us. And I have a big surprise baked into my plan. I love surprises, don't you? And I assure you, this surprise is practically foolproof." Then Madame brandished her lightsaber, and with a sweeping glowing motion, she held it close to Thaddeus's neck. "So long as there are no *fools* on the team. Understand?"

Even though Thaddeus knew Madame X wasn't actually there, he still felt like the lightsaber might burn through his carotid artery. "I-I-I understand, Madame," he stammered.

Madame X retracted the lightsaber. "Good, Thaddeus. "Keep it up. The stars and planets must be aligned, *literally*, for our little trip. We can't be a minute to soon or late."

"Yes, Madame."

With one last giant inhale, Madame X vanished.

Just then, Thaddeus's cell phone rang. He pulled it from his pocket and glanced at the screen. It was Wainright. Thaddeus answered the call, hoping for good news. "Did you find what we're looking for?"

"Not yet," Wainright said. "But we think we know who may have Proto."

Thaddeus listened intently. "Who?"

"Jason Pascal. Dr. Pascal's twelve-year-old son."

Thaddeus swiveled in his chair to look at the monitor that showed Dr. Pascal hard at work. *Her son?*

"How did he—" Thaddeus began to feel his temperature rise. A twelve-year-old boy was causing life-and-death delays? *A kid?!*

"It appears Dr. Pascal made Jason's little field trip to Recode Global more educational than she was supposed to. We were able to secure video footage that shows Jason entering the lab alone and leaving just before we had planned to remove Proto from the lab."

Thaddeus clenched his teeth. He might have underestimated Dr. Pascal's intelligence. Maybe she knew what was about to take place and had Jason nab Proto.

"Dooley is still trying to find a back door into Proto so he can locate it," Wainright continued. "But none of Dr. Pascal's protocols are working. We think she might have set up a fail-safe measure in the event Proto ever left the lab without authorization."

Dr. Pascal *was* outsmarting them, right before his very eyes. She had sworn up and down that the protocols she had given them would work.

"What do you want us to do?" Wainright asked.

"Isn't it obvious?" Thaddeus seethed.

"Torture Dr. Pascal?" Wainright offered.

"No, you idiot," Thaddeus said. "Get the boy, with or without Proto. It seems Dr. Pascal might need a little more incentive to do her job well."

"Anything else, boss?"

"Yeah, tell Dr. Pascal that we need to show a miracle of progress by tomorrow and set a timer that makes it clear when she needs to be done. If she doesn't finish by the time it goes off, she'll have to face the consequences."

Or both of us will, Thaddeus thought as he wiped his brow.

From Madame X.

INTO BATTLE WITH NO COMBAT TRAINING

Not long after Jason made the call to Maya, the door-bell rang. Jason ordered Proto to stay behind as he bounded down the stairs to answer it. "I'll get it!" he hollered.

"Thanks, dear," Aunt Dotty called from the kitchen.

Jason opened the door, then held a finger to his lips as soon as he saw Maya, backpack on, standing on his stoop. Her bike was resting alongside the house.

"Let me do the talking," Jason whispered. "Otherwise, Aunt Dotty will talk your ear off."

"Aunt Dotty!" Jason called, "Maya's here. We're going to park her bike in the garage and get to work!"

"Sounds good," Aunt Dotty replied. "I'll call you when dinner is ready."

When Jason and Maya got to Jason's room, Proto was doing something that looked like gymnastics on Jason's bed.

Proto paused. "Hello, Maya."

"Hey, Proto," Maya said.

Jason shut the door. "What on Earth are you doing?"

"I was just learning the art of Wing Chun kung fu," Proto explained. "Did you know that Wing Chun was taught to the famous Bruce Lee? You can immobilize your fiercest competitors if you are skilled in the art."

"Uh," Maya said. "You do realize you weigh less than five ounces, right?"

"Mind over matter, my dear Maya," Proto said.

Maya dropped her backpack to the floor and sat at Jason's desk. "So, what did the FBI say about your mom?"

Jason sat beside Proto and filled Maya in, from his mom's unknown whereabouts to the possibility that she might even be in on Proto's disappearance.

"That's ridiculous," Maya said. "Proto left with you by accident. Why didn't you just tell them what happened?"

Jason raised an eyebrow. "Think about it. If suspicious people took my mom, and no one knows where she is, who can I trust?"

Maya frowned. "Um . . . the FBI?"

Jason shook his head. "No, something about that guy didn't seem totally right. Right, Proto?"

"He did have indigestion," Proto confirmed.

"Indigestion?" Maya groaned. "That doesn't make him untrustworthy."

"Listen, Maya," Jason said, "I didn't rule him out entirely. I told him everything I knew about Pinky and King Kong, but I saw no need to tell them about Proto's whereabouts. What if he's after Proto? He won't care about my mom."

"What about Dr. Cooper?" Maya said. "Did he seem strange?"

Proto piped in. "He's got asthma, poor hearing, and, like me, admires Patty."

"Dr. Cooper just wants his billion-dollar device back," Jason explained. "I doubt he really cares about Mom either."

Maya say quietly for a minute. "I see what you mean. Okay, so don't be offended if I ask this, but are you sure your mother isn't on the wrong side of this?"

Jason stared at her. "I'm as sure about my mom as . . . as the sky being blue."

"Actually," Proto said, "the atmosphere is transparent. It only appears to be blue due to the process of Rayleigh scattering. When the sun's light passes through gas molecules in our atmosphere—"

"Proto, really?" Jason interrupted. "Can you just not do that?"

"Do what?" Proto asked. "Am I not being helpful?"

"Never mind."

"I was also going to add," Proto continued, "that I am 99.6 percent certain Dr. Shannon Pascal is an honest, law-abiding citizen. She would not have any plans to steal me."

"That's specific," Maya said. "How do you know that?"

"I arrived at this figure taking numerous factors about Dr. Pascal's history into account. These include her voting and driving records, school attendance from elementary through doctorate level, her Myers-Briggs personality test results, and her owning the world's third-largest Muppet doll collection. I find learning about Dr. Pascal and then comparing her to the human population to create predictive models quite thrilling."

"Wait, what?" Maya said. "Did you say Muppets?"

"Yeah, it's this whole . . . thing." Jason shrugged. "She lent her collection to a museum."

"Oh-kay," Maya said. "Why 99.6 percent and not 100 percent? And how do you know all that stuff about Dr. Pascal?"

"Dr. Pascal has spent many hours educating me on herself and the topics of empathy and human personality. I gave her a 99.6 percent confidence score based on an incident of illegal parking twelve years and four months ago, which resulted in her vehicle being towed away."

"Got it," Maya said. "It sure doesn't sound like your mom would try to help get Proto into the wrong hands."

"We have to think about our leads," Jason said, pacing the floor. "That's what detectives do, right, Maya? We know King Kong has a connection to Al's Trucks, so that's definitely suspicious. We should find out where King Kong, I mean, *Todd Wainright*, lives."

"Yes!" Maya said. "Proto, see if you can find an address for Todd Wainright, his dad, or even that Dooley woman."

Proto glowed. "A public records search yields one property result for Al Wainright, Todd's father. He purchased a two-story home located in the Country Meadows subdivision of Button—" Suddenly Proto's light flashed and he let out a loud squawk.

Maya and Jason both covered their ears.

"What was that, Proto?" Jason asked.

"Jason? Maya?" Aunt Dotty called. "Everything okay?"

"Sorry, Aunt Dotty, it's part of our project!" Jason called back. "Turning down the volume now!" He turned to Proto. "Are you all right?"

"My apologies," Proto said. "I received an odd communication. I believe I may have just been contacted by an artificial intelligence bearing my own signature."

"Wait, what?" Maya said. "Another AI? I thought you were the only prototype."

"I thought so, too," Proto said. "I have just received images via my own internal communication channels." Proto displayed the images in the center of the bedroom: a workroom with a messy desk covered in assorted high-tech tools, a mechanical watch shell, metallic rods, tiny components for electronic circuits, and Jason's mother reading a Chinese take-out menu.

"Mom!" Jason said. He had never been happier to see her face, or at least the part that wasn't covered by the menu she was holding.

"She must have figured out a way to contact Proto," Maya said.

"Then she's alive!" Jason said. "But why the menu? Mom doesn't even like Chinese food."

"That's gotta be a clue," Maya said. "Quick, look at the other pictures. The watch casing, the metal rods . . . seem familiar?"

Jason glanced at Proto. "Yeah."

"I am made out of many of those components," Proto confirmed. "It appears she is making another prototype, which explains how Dr. Pascal might have contacted me in the manner that she did."

"I bet the menu is a clue since it's so out of place," Jason said. "Proto, zoom in on the menu."

Proto enlarged the menu so it was easier to read.

"Chao's Chow," Jason read. "I know that restaurant. It's in Groveland, the next town over."

"Look!" Maya pointed at the projection of the menu. "The delivery boundaries are right on there. Proto, pull up a map of that area."

Proto displayed an image that displayed the restaurant's delivery zone alongside the image of Jason's mother. Jason scanned the territory; there were a few subdivisions of houses, some small strip malls with fast food restaurants, and a warehouse on the edge.

"That has to be where's she at," Jason said. "All that equipment. Her work area. The tall ceilings. Are you thinking what I'm thinking, Maya?"

"The warehouse," Jason and Maya said in unison.

"Who does the warehouse belong to?" Jason got a sinking feeling in his stomach. "Proto, find out."

"It is owned by TechToy Industries," Proto announced.

Maya gasped. "I know that company."

"So do I," Jason said.

All three of them turned to stare at Patty sitting on Jason's desk.

Jason's earlier conversations with his mother about the toy loomed large in his head. *That company isn't pro-social*, his mother had said.

Now Jason understood what she had meant.

TechToy Industries wasn't pro-social at all. It was doing things that would be bad for society. *Very bad.*

"I bet TechToy is just a facade for some devious plan," Maya said. "Like how the mafia uses restaurants to launder money."

"Pinky and King Kong probably work for TechToy," Jason added. "At least it looks that way. Zoom out on Mom's image again. Maybe there are more clues. When was the photo taken? Can you tell?"

"The metadata for the image reads five minutes and seventeen seconds ago."

"That's good," Jason said. "Hopefully that means she's still okay."

Maya gasped. "Check out the digital clock on the wall behind her. That doesn't show the time. It's almost 6:00 p.m. now, but that says 12:54. If she's in Groveland, she can't be in another time zone."

"No, Maya," Proto said. "There is no time zone that is six minutes less of the hour."

Jason's mouth went dry as he realized what the clock was. "That's not a time-telling clock. That's a countdown clock."

"You're right, Jason," Maya said. "It looks like the kind of timer they put on bombs."

Proto's glow turned orange. *Bombs?* Are we hypothesizing that in twelve hours and fifty-four minutes, Dr. Pascal will explode?"

"Proto, don't jump to conclusions," Jason said. "We don't know what will happen when that time runs out. Maybe that's Mom's deadline to make them another prototype?"

"That is a sound hypothesis," Proto said.

"Can you talk back to whatever was talking to you, Proto?" Jason asked.

"Wait!" Maya said. "Don't do that, Proto. We don't know for sure who or what is sending us those messages. What if it's a trap to find Proto? We have to call the authorities now, Jason."

"If we can't trust whomever is sending us these messages," Jason said firmly, "then we can't trust anyone. Especially the authorities."

"Call your dad," Maya said. "He can help."

"No, he'll just tell Agent Sparks," Jason replied. "Dad will blab. I guarantee it."

"Jason is correct," Proto said. "Mr. Pascal has already agreed to share everything he knows with Agent Sparks."

"So what can we do then?" Maya said.

"Through the process of elimination," Proto said, "there appear to be only three entities that can help Dr. Pascal. You, Jason, and me."

"Then we have no choice but to go in *ourselves*." Jason rose from the bed and picked up Patty from his desk. He studied the DronePro as if he was trying to get to know his enemy.

"Go in?" Maya said. "Uh, we are two twelve-year-olds who have no combat training whatsoever. How are we supposed to go up against trained brainiac bad guys holding your mother hostage?"

Jason didn't know, but he suspected the answer to Maya's question might be found with the DronePro. Patty was well-made, sturdy, and light, a feat of engineering. A plan began to formulate in his mind.

"Jason?" Maya said. "*Hellooo*, how do you suppose we do this without getting nabbed ourselves?"

"Maya is right," Proto added. "You should not attempt to retrieve your mother on your own. The two of you were unable to handle dogs much smaller than lunch boxes."

Jason set down the DronePro. "Maya, we have to take your own advice."

Maya stared at him. "Huh?"

"Don't you remember?" Jason said. "We have the best armor around to protect us *and* my mother."

"Wait, Jason," Proto said. "Do you mean . . . *me?*" He glowed pink.

Maya looked like she was thinking it over. "That's true." Her voice became calmer. "We do have Proto."

Proto continued to glow. "I am so glad I can be of service."

"We'll need to prepare," Jason said. "Proto can help us with that. If that is a countdown clock, then Mom still has time, and so do we."

Jason picked up Patty again. "I have an idea. Follow me."

101 WAYS TO TORTURE YOUR LITTLE BROTHER

Proto wrapped himself around Jason's wrist as Jason held Patty and led Maya into the hall. "Aunt Dotty!" Jason called out. "We're going to the basement to set up our project there."

"Okay, sweetie," she yelled back. "Dinner will be ready soon. I hope you're hungry!"

Jason led Maya down a different set of stairs, across a large recreation room, and through a thick door at the far end. They hurried down a dark concrete corridor.

"Where are we going?" Maya asked. "The center of the Earth?"

"Like I said," Jason told her, "we need to prepare." He paused in front of a thick metal door at the end of the corridor. "My mom convinced Dad that we should have a fully operational underground bunker in case of a disaster. It also doubles as Mom's home office."

He handed Patty to Maya, then used both hands to push the heavy door inward, revealing a DIY scientist's dream. Inside, dozens of machines and computers sat atop long metal tables. Tools of all types hung on the walls. Cabinets and drawers were filled with supplies, and counters lining the perimeter of the room held more devices and machines that were beyond Jason's understanding. The place even had its own sitting area with couches and a rug. "Mom lets me hang out here sometimes to watch a movie with her since that wall over there is the biggest screen in the house. Her only rule is that I don't touch anything."

Maya set Patty down on one of the lab tables. "Why do I have a feeling we're going to be breaking that rule?"

"I am having the same thought," Proto said.

"I figure Mom won't mind now, given the circumstances."

"Well then . . ." Proto jumped off of Jason's wrist and landed next to Patty. He made a realistic-sounding whistle. "This is a wonderful place!" He leaped from surface to surface to check everything out. "This feels—this feels like *home* to me! I love it!"

Maya walked around the lab. "Your mom's, like . . . Batwoman, and this is her Batcave."

"So here's the plan," Jason said. "I figure if our bad guys can engineer a useful toy like Patty, then Proto certainly could build us better stuff."

"Clever, Jason," Maya said. "Beat them at their own game, a classic crime-fighting maneuver."

Proto bounded onto the table. "I am creating plans as we speak." His light pulsed as though he was performing billions of calculations. "There are so many choices." He projected images of tanks, fighter planes, missiles . . .

"Hold up," Maya said. "We are *not* going to build jets and launch missiles."

"Yeah," Jason agreed. "Proto, the objective is to protect us, not kill. Let's think about what can make in a few hours, tops, that's totally street-legal, okay?"

"Ah, thank you for constraining my parameters, Jason." Proto paused for barely a second. Then he flashed up larger-than-life images of makeshift weapons designed for deterrence and distraction. "I must admit I found a very intriguing article online called, *101 Ways to Torture Your Little Brother Without Doing Permanent Damage: A Guide for Handy Children Who Love Science.* I can modify these ideas to make them more powerful without causing additional harm."

"Perfect," Maya said, staring at what looked like a home-made rocket launcher. "Does that thing catapult fruit?!"

Jason studied another image of a device that looked like a powerful magnet that could stick small children to refrigerators. "That could come in handy."

"There is some bad news, however," Proto said. "Your mother's lab does not have everything we need." He flashed up a list of materials that included screws, chemicals, piping, and other miscellaneous items. "But Hardware Land is just a few miles away."

"Aunt Dotty can take us," Jason said. "That'll be faster."

Aunt Dotty was thrilled Jason and Maya would ask for her help on their "science project." She cheerfully put dinner-making on pause, and it wasn't long before Jason, with Proto in his pocket, and Maya piled into the back of Aunt Dotty's station wagon.

The sun was beginning to set as Aunt Dotty backed the car out of the driveway. As they headed toward their destination, Jason's mind filled with thoughts about his mom. Was she okay? Would they get to her in time?

"We're here!" Aunt Dotty announced, pulling into Hardware Land's parking lot. Just as Aunt Dotty put the car in park, Jason and Maya jumped out. "If you need me," Aunty Dotty called after, "I'll be looking for a new houseplant in the gardening section."

Inside, Jason and Maya stared at dozens of rows of shelves overflowing with anything anybody could ever want to build practically everything.

"Proto," Jason whispered, "tell us what we need."

Proto rattled off a list of supplies in Jason's ear as Maya pushed around a cart, going from one aisle to the next to locate each item. Everything was in stock: piping, screws, wires, foam, special glues and compounds, a rare pepper plant in the gardening section, and backpacks to carry it all. Only one item to go. "Where does a hardware store put magnesium chloride?" Jason asked.

"Hardware Land's website shows the material is categorized under landscaping," Proto said, "as ice melt."

"Shoot," Maya said. "Weren't we just there? I didn't see any ice melt. Did you? We'll have to ask someone."

Jason remembered seeing a man wearing a trucker's cap and a Hardware Land apron pass by at the other end of the aisle. "Stay here, Maya. I saw someone who can help." He hurried down the aisle and turned the corner. The man was standing a few aisles away. His back was turned to him, and he was stacking small boxes onto a shelf. Jason started toward him.

"Jason," Proto said, "I am detecting a familiar biorhythmic pattern—"

Jason paused. "Bio-what?" he whispered.

"Biorhythmic, defined as regular, recurring—"

Jason rolled his eyes. "Proto, not now, please." He had magnesium chloride to find. He closed the gap between himself and the man and tapped him on the shoulder. "Excuse me, sir."

The man didn't turn. Instead he grabbed a nearby box of nails and hid his face before Jason could see it. "Look, kid." His voice sounded ridiculously low. "I'm busy."

Jason backed up. Something about the guy seemed very wrong.

"Jason," Proto said, "I am trying to tell you that that is not a Hardware Land employee. That's—"

"Who are you?" Jason said loudly. A little too loudly. If he had just run into a bad guy, he was not going to go quietly. A female customer at the end of the aisle was examining door hardware. She stopped to look at them.

The man sighed. He lowered the box of nails. "Keep your voice down or you'll blow my cover."

"Agent Sparks?" Jason said.

"Agent Sparks," Proto confirmed. "Jason, at some point, we need to talk about when I can talk to help you in certain situations. My timing appears to be off far too often."

Just then, Maya's voice rang out. "Jason, what's going on?"

Jason turned. Maya was standing with their shopping cart at the end of the aisle he'd just left.

"Great, just great," Agent Sparks said.

Jason attempted to wave her away.

But she misread his signal and started coming toward them. "Did you find the ice melt?"

"Remember what I said about being discreet?" Agent Sparks whispered. "Your little friend can't know who I am."

Jason narrowed his eyes. The one thing he did know was that he didn't have to take orders from someone he didn't trust. "Are you spying on us?"

Maya joined them. "Spying?" Her voice turned serious as she looked from Jason to Agent Sparks. "Jason, what's going on?"

"Lower your voice, little girl," Agent Sparks said.

"*Little* girl?" Maya said, raising an eyebrow. "Why should I lower my voice? Who is this guy?"

The lady in the door hardware section began to seem concerned for Jason and Maya. "Children?" she called. "Do you need some help?"

Agent Sparks immediately started shelving nails and talking through the side of his mouth. "If you two don't quit it, you're going to draw attention to me, and if you're being watched, and they know who I am, you could ruin the entire operation. Do you understand?"

Jason looked from Maya to the agent. Maybe he was a real agent. He sure sounded like one. "We're doing fine," Jason called to the woman. "Just looking for some ice melt!"

She smiled back and went back to whatever she was doing.

Agent Sparks started walking in the opposite direction of the woman. "Follow me," he whispered.

"We're being watched?" Maya whispered back.

"Yeah, by me," Agent Sparks replied. "That's my job. And who knows who else you don't want to meet."

"Wait," Jason said, "Aren't you supposed to be with my dad? Where is he?"

"At the field office. He's fine. Now stop talking about this." Agent Sparks then spoke in a regular, super-friendly Hardware Land-employee type of voice. "Kids, did you say you're looking for ice melt?"

"Yeah," Jason said, cooperating for the time being. "It's for a science project."

"Follow me," Agent Sparks replied. They passed aisle after aisle of hardware and browsing customers. He stopped in front of a section that Jason and Maya had missed in landscaping. "Right where I thought it was." Agent Sparks picked up a large container and threw it into the cart. "Good luck with your project!" Then he lowered his voice. "Now scram. I mean it. Stay at home. Don't make my job any harder than it already is."

"Jason!" Aunt Dotty called from the gardening section nearby. She was holding a bamboo plant in her arms. "Are you two finished?"

"Yeah," Jason said. "We'll meet you at checkout." Then he turned to Agent Sparks and matched his tone. "Stay away from us," he whispered. "Maybe *we* need to be watching *you.*"

"Good one," Maya said approvingly. Then without looking back, Jason and Maya pushed their cart toward the front of the store and joined Jason's aunt at the registers.

When they returned to the house, night had fallen. Jason and Maya lugged their Hardware Land items inside as Aunt Dotty went to finish making dinner. Just before Jason shut the front door, he considered what Agent Sparks had said about being watched. He studied the street. Nothing seemed odd about the neighborhood. The usual cars that belonged to neighbors were parked outside. Mr. Conway, a neighbor who lived down the street, jogged by on his usual pre-dinner run, and Jason could hear the Zalinskis' yappy dog across the street.

Before he shut the door, he wondered if Agent Sparks was still surveilling them somehow.

"Dinner will be ready in about fifteen minutes," Aunt Dotty said from the kitchen. "Now do your best not to blow up the basement while I try not to burn the apple pie."

Once the door to Dr. Pascal's lab was firmly closed behind them, Jason pulled Proto out of his pocket and set him on a lab table.

"Finally," Proto said. "I have seen much cleaner places than your pocket."

"Sorry about that," Jason said. He and Maya began unloading their supplies onto a large lab table in the middle of the room.

"So, what did you think of Agent Sparks, Proto?" Jason said.

"I was about to ask you the same question," Proto said. He began to pace the table's surface with his eight tiny legs, just like Jason had earlier in his room. "I cannot tell if he is a legitimate government agent or not. The FBI does not make the employee roster available online, and he showed no physical signs of deception. However," Proto spun around and walked in the opposite direction. "FBI agents are also trained to deceive, as you saw in the store. It's an interesting conundrum." He turned once more and kept talking. "And that brings me to the other issue I want to discuss—when exactly should I speak to you when I have something important to tell you?" He stopped in the center of the table, surrounded by their miscellaneous supplies.

"Oh yeah, that," Jason said. "This one-way communication thing can be such a pain. I wish there was a way you could just read my mind. It would make things so much easier."

Proto glowed yellow. "That's an excellent idea. I will work on figuring that out."

"Good luck," Jason said. "And since we don't have any clear idea about Agent Sparks, there's no reason we should tell him anything, right? Maya?"

"Right," Maya said. "I would trust anybody *but* him. He's so weird." She started gathering up empty bags. "Okay, everything is all out. Let's get started."

"Wait," Proto said. "Before we begin, I must warn you that you must respect the materials you use and the devices you are making, or you could get hurt, at least temporarily."

"No problem," Jason said.

"Proto," Maya said, "you're good at being parental."

"Dr. Pascal programmed me, after all," he answered proudly. "I would be honored to have any of her best qualities. Maya, why don't you get that PVC pipe and begin with the air cannon?" He projected a holographic diagram with step-by-step instructions to show her what to do.

Maya put the tube in a worktable clamp and got to work.

"Jason, input these parameters into the 3D printer on the counter." Proto projected a list for him. "Then grab those black sheets. Those are made of carbon nanotubes, an incredibly strong and versatile material we can use to construct nano-velcro. But we only have a small quantity, so do not mess up."

"Thanks for the vote of confidence," Jason said. "I got this."

"You have to plug in the 3D printer first," Proto said.

"I knew that."

All three worked hard at assembling their weapons of mass distraction. Proto's holo-instructions were very specific, which kept Jason from mistakenly setting off the smoke bombs he had made or Maya from accidentally triggering the expanding sticky-foam "Mammoth's Toothpaste" she had concocted.

Proto painstakingly wrapped copper wiring around the iron rod before having Maya hook it up to a portable battery for charging. "The Irresistible Magno-Rod can only be discharged once," Proto said. "Use it wisely."

Each time Jason thought he had made the coolest thing, Proto had him switch to an even better contraption. Patty was still sitting on the table. The DronePro now seemed totally uncool in comparison. "Is there any way we can still use Patty for our cause?" Jason asked.

"Absolutely," Proto said. "As a flying vehicle, I'm sure Patty will be useful."

"I love the idea of using their own stuff against them," Maya said. "Pinky and King Kong won't see us coming."

"Proto," Jason said, "you're like our portable mad scientist."

There was a knock on the lab door.

Everyone froze.

"I brought dinner down," Aunt Dotty said, her voice muffled by the door. "Wow, it's so strange down here. What's with the tunnel?"

Jason looked around the room filled with the makings of their weapons. Aunt Dotty couldn't see any of this! Maya seemed to be thinking the same thing, judging by the way she was trying to throw her body over the lab table's contents.

"Aunt Dotty," Jason called. "If you could just leave it outside, we'll eat in a sec. We don't want to lose momentum."

"Sure thing, honey," Aunt Dotty replied. "But come upstairs for the pie when that's out. Your food is already getting cold down here."

"We wouldn't miss pie," Jason said.

Aunt Dotty's footsteps faded away.

Jason and Maya breathed a collective sigh of relief.

"Please eat," Proto said. "You will need your energy. While you do that, I have one more thing I want to finish."

Jason didn't think he could eat at a time like this, but after giving the thought a second to play in his mind, he realized he was starved. "Good idea."

Jason opened the door, grabbed the TV tray Aunt Dotty had left outside, and brought it into the lab.

"That smells so good!" Maya said.

Jason and Maya began to chow down as Proto manipulated some materials from Dr. Pascal's lab to finish his own small project. "*Señor y señorita! Mira eso!*"

"*Mira eso?*" Jason said.

Maya paused between bites of spaghetti. "That's Spanish. He said, 'Look at that!'"

"You speak Spanish, too?" Proto asked.

"Yeah," Maya replied. "My parents are from Mexico. My mom was a real stickler about keeping the language in our family, so I can read and write in Spanish, too."

"Cool," Jason said, impressed.

Proto and Maya began to talk about something in Spanish, and he found himself wishing his parents had taught him more than Bike-Speak and Science-Talk.

Jason interrupted their conversation. "You better not be making fun of me, Proto."

Maya laughed. "Proto was just telling me that he had made something for me."

"*Sí*," Proto said. Then he held up a modified Bluetooth earpiece. "This is for Maya."

"For me?" Maya said. "I get my own earpiece?" She took the earpiece from Proto and stuck it in her ear.

"How does it feel?" Proto asked. "How do I sound?"

"*Muy bien!*" Maya said. "It's like you're right inside my ear."

Proto glowed blue. "I am getting quite good at figuring out how to modify existing schematics to execute enhancements. It won't be long before I am completely inventing things on my own through self-learning."

"Wow," Jason said, "Now two people get to hear all of your interesting words, Proto."

Proto laughed, a deep, rich belly laugh that couldn't possibly come out of a body that small. "Do I detect sarcasm, Jason?"

"You *are* learning, Proto," Maya said. "Just yesterday you wouldn't have even noticed."

Proto's glow turned pink. "That's what I was programmed to do. I learn. Though I must admit I am a bit disappointed. I had hoped to figure out how to read your minds by now, but my neural network has not quite solved that problem yet. Perhaps more experiences will give me new revelations about how I can use the data that I have."

Maya gaped. "Are you serious? You can really learn how to read minds?"

"What *can't* he learn?" Jason said "That's the real question."

Before Proto could answer, a buzzing sound went off through the lab.

"What's that?" Maya asked.

"The doorbell," Jason said, immediately feeling tense. He put down his food and rose from the table. "My mom set up a camera so she could answer the door from her lab."

"Probably Agents Sparks snooping on us," Maya said.

"Ugh." Jason got up and tapped a button marked VIDEO on a nearby screen.

Sure enough, the monitor showed Agent Sparks greeting Aunt Dotty at the door, except this time he was holding up an official-looking FBI badge for Aunt Dotty to see.

"That's weird," Jason said. "Agent Sparks said it was best to keep the case discreet."

"That's definitely not discreet," Maya said.

Jason tapped AUDIO to listen in.

"Ms. Dotty Pascal?" Agent Sparks said. "I'm afraid we have reason to believe that you and anyone else in this home could be in danger."

"What's this about?" Aunt Dotty said. "Is this about my brother? He said he was coming home, not more than half an hour ago."

"Actually, it is." Agent Sparks made a move to come in, but Aunt Dotty stood fast. "There are children in this house, sir. If Ray is in trouble—"

Jason couldn't believe his ears. *Dad?* Something had happened to Dad?

"Ma'am, there's no time to discuss this now. Gather the children, then we'll get you all to a safe place. We'll talk about it then."

"I don't like the sound of this," Maya said. "We're all going to get kidnapped."

"We got to get out of here," Jason said, even though he wanted to call his dad. But there was no time. "Now, now!" He started gathering up whatever weapons he could fit in their backpacks. "Come on, Maya, get everything you can."

Maya grabbed everything she could reach and started stuffing things into her backpack. She strapped Patty to the outside of it. "What about your aunt?"

"My aunt?" Jason paused. He looked at the screen.

Aunt Dotty was still refusing to let Agent Sparks in. "But didn't Ray go with *you*?" she said. "Where's Ray?"

Proto jumped onto Jason's wrist. "Your aunt seems very distressed, as does Agent Sparks."

"Ma'am!" Agent Sparks said more forcefully. "If you do not listen to federal orders, I have the right to arrest you. Am I making myself clear?"

Aunt Dotty held fast. "Tell me where my brother is!"

"Ma'am, if you would just cooperate." He moved toward her.

"Don't you dare lay a hand on me!" Aunt Dotty shouted. "What did you do to my brother?!" She gave Agent Sparks a hard shove as if to protect herself. "Kids," she called. "Run!"

Suddenly, Agent Sparks reached around Aunt Dotty and put her in a neck hold. "Let it be known that you have just assaulted a federal officer," he said. "I am within my rights to subdue you."

Maya screamed. Jason stared at the monitor, dumbfounded.

Aunt Dotty went limp in seconds.

Agent Sparks looked in the direction of the camera. "Kids, I know you're watching. She's just unconscious. We need to get out of here right now. I'm here to help. You have to believe me."

"Heck no," Jason said, seeing his limp Aunt in Sparks's arms. "We have to go!"

Jason hurried to the far side of the lab for the emergency exit, but Maya didn't move.

"If it helps," Proto said in Jason's and Maya's ears, "I do believe Aunt Dotty is unconscious like Agent Sparks said. I detected chest movements from breathing after he loosened his hold on her."

"Oh no," Maya said. "Sparks just pulled your aunt inside the house with him."

"Maya," Jason said, "stop looking at the video. Let's *go!*"

Maya snapped out of it, and moments later Jason opened the emergency exit door, which let them out toward the back of the yard, hidden in trees. Jason's heart was pounding. He stared at his house. The lights came on through an upstairs window. Jason could see Agent Sparks's shadow moving from room to room. "Our bikes. We gotta get them." He and Maya hurried through the moonlit darkness, entered the side door of the garage, and wheeled them out.

"We have to get to the woods," Jason whispered. "It's the easiest place to hide until we figure out what to do."

They jumped on their bikes with all of their gear, turned on their headlights, and pedaled like mad across the street.

They passed a blue sedan parked quietly on the street. The car's motor roared to life, and its headlights blinked on.

WE'RE IN TOO DEEP

"Who's that!?" Maya said, looking back at the car. "I thought Sparks was in your house!"

Jason and Maya biked down the path that cut through the field to get to the trailhead. "He has a team," Jason said. "Remember?"

The car gave chase, jumping the curb.

"Oh, great!" Maya said.

"Just pedal," Jason ordered.

The sound of the car behind them grew to a deafening sound.

"Jason, Maya," Proto said. "Pedal faster. You have an 82 percent chance of making it to the trailhead before the car if you do not lose speed."

"I'm going, I'm going!" Maya said, keeping pace right alongside Jason.

Jason could see the trailhead coming into view. His bulky backpack bounced awkwardly against his back, threatening his balance.

"If you make it," Proto said, "take the Danforth Trail to the right. It is mostly rocky, but downhill, which will increase your momentum."

Jason could see the trailhead sign now. He heard the car groan to a halt.

The sound of car doors slamming and angry shouting helped Jason push even harder.

"Stop!" a man's voice bellowed.

Jason and Maya's bikes rode into the tree line.

"Don't stop!" Jason panted. His muscles burned as he dodged trees and rode down bumps, roots, and rocks.

"Don't worry!" Maya panted back. She pulled ahead of Jason.

Maya took the trail right at the fork, with Jason close behind. Proto then displayed a magnificent light of his own, highlighting a dirt path for Maya and Jason that would let them pick up even more speed.

"Jason," Proto said, "*Duck!*"

Jason immediately obeyed and heard a whistling sound. Something zoomed over his head and struck the tree in front of him. As Jason pedaled past, he glimpsed a silvery cord sparking with electricity.

"What was that?" Jason asked, struggling to speak.

"Some sort of electrical *bola*," Proto said. "Also called *boleadoras*, it's a South American tool that uses weighted cords to entangle prey without killing it. Except this was modified to discharge electricity."

"Fabulous," Jason said.

"Maya, please do not get too far in front of Jason," Proto said. "My display is far less effective if I have to disperse light a longer distance with more physical impediments between the two of you."

"I'm. Not. *That.* Far. Behind," Jason managed.

Soon it became obvious that they had left their pursuers behind. All they could hear was the sound of their bikes traversing the path, deep into the woods.

After a few more minutes, Proto announced they could rest. "We have traveled far enough that any on-foot pursuit would be miles behind. Turn off your headlamps."

Jason and Maya slowed to a stop, grateful for a break. They dismounted, switched off their headlamps, and leaned their bikes against the trees. They sat on the ground to catch their breath.

Slowly, Jason's eyes adjusted to the moonlight filtering in through the trees. "Who—who were the people who tried to electrocute me?" Jason said, his voice ragged.

Proto climbed onto his knee. "My voice analysis indicates one voice was likely male and the other voice female."

"Female?" Jason said. "I didn't even realize there was a woman after us. I only heard the guy."

"Pinky and King Kong?" Maya asked.

"Possibly," Proto replied, "but I have no way to confirm this since I do not have a recording of their voices for comparison. Pinky and King Kong had been silent when we saw them with your mother, Jason."

"We can't stay here long," Jason said. "We have to get to the warehouse."

Maya nodded, though she didn't speak. She turned her face away from Jason.

"Maya," Jason said. "Are you okay?"

"I'm sorry," Maya blubbered. "I still can't shake the image of your aunt getting *subdued*. And what about your dad, Jason?" She turned to look at him. "He went with Agent Sparks, who might not be so good after all! How are you even functioning?"

Dad. He pulled his phone from his pocket, tempted to call him.

He looked at Maya. Could he call him? Would it make things worse?

"I wouldn't do that," Maya said, as though knowing what he was thinking. "We can't talk to anyone. Turn off your phone." She grabbed it from him and switched it off. "It has GPS. They can track us through that."

She returned Jason's phone to him and pulled out her own phone to power it off. A tear slid down her cheek as she stared at the dark screen. "Bye, Mom. Bye, Dad."

Oh no, Jason thought. "No, no, no, no." Jason put his hands up. "Please, don't do that." Seeing Maya like that only made him feel horribly guilty and even worse than before.

Maya wiped away her tears. "I'm sorry, I'm sorry," she blurted. "I didn't mean to, I just—"

"Actually, Maya," Proto said. "Weeping is a natural human response to events of sadness and joy. I think . . ." Proto paused. Then his glow dimmed. "I think . . ."

Proto went dark.

Jason heard him make a sniffling sound.

"Not you too, Proto!" Jason begged. "Please stop. We can cry when we know there is something to really cry about. But not now, okay? For all we know, everyone is alive and totally savable. We have to think positive."

Proto's glow slowly came back. "Yes, you are right, Jason. Dr. Pascal has told me this before."

Proto climbed up Jason's arm and sat on his shoulder. "Listen." Proto played back a recording of Dr. Pascal's voice. "We must think positive, Proto," she said. "Have hope. We must have hope for humanity."

Hearing his mother's voice made Jason's eyes well up. "When did she say this to you, Proto?"

"The day I was activated," Proto said, "I will never forget. I shall have hope for Dr. Pascal, Aunt Dotty, and your father."

"Thank you," Jason said. He grew quiet, knowing his mother would want him to stay strong and have hope, just like she had said. "Listen, Maya, if you wanna go home, you can. I would totally understand."

Maya shook her head. "No, that won't help. I'm already involved, and they know it. Besides, none of that matters." She took in a deep breath and let it out.

Jason was confused. "How come?"

"Because . . ." Maya wiped her face then stood up. "Your mom needs us. Your family needs us." She put on her backpack. "And I'm your friend, Jason. We need to go. How much time do we have left, Proto?"

"Ten hours, fifty minutes, and five seconds," Proto said.

Jason looked up at Maya. "Thanks, Maya."

He didn't know what he had done to deserve a friend like her, but he wasn't going to complain.

"All in a day's work." She held out her hand to help him up.

He took it and got to his feet.

He knew he couldn't do this without her.

13

A HOTBED OF NEFARIOUS CORPORATE ACTIVITY

Jason and Maya got on their bikes. Jason adjusted his backpack, then followed the trail according to Proto's directions. About thirty-five minutes later, they approached the warehouse. Jason and Maya were careful to stay as far from view as possible. They leaned their bikes against a dumpster at the far end of the parking lot and peeked around it to get a good look at the building.

TechToy's manufacturing facility looked normal for a warehouse—two stories, hardly any windows. Not a single car was in the surface lot.

"Crazy quiet," Maya said, "isn't it? Doesn't exactly look like a hotbed of nefarious corporate activity."

"How are we supposed to get in?" Jason said. "I can already see a few security cameras from here."

"Elementary, my dear, Watson!" Proto said, taking on a British accent. "I am quite fascinated by Sir Arthur Conan Doyle's Sherlock Holmes stories and the subsequent films. I have deduced the following—"

"Deduce faster, Proto, okay?" Jason said. "We don't have all day."

"Yes, I'll get to the point," Proto said. "Holmes once said, 'We must look for the things we cannot see.' Now this led me to realize that if I can sense nuances within the electrical network that powers this building, assuming the security cameras are wired, which almost all good systems are—unless our enemies are very naïve, which is doubtful—then I can detect where each camera is positioned even if I cannot see them."

"Wow," Maya said. "That's clever."

"It's all just a matter of current and frequencies," Proto said. He flashed up an image of the building with hot spots marked all over it. "There's a point of vulnerability here. This side of the building has a dead space that is not surveilled for some reason." He zoomed in on the east side of the building and outlined a structure connected below it. "That big dark space underground is also not in the building plans that were filed with the city."

"Wait," Maya said. "What? This place has a secret chamber?"

"Yes," Proto zeroed in on a section that had no hotspots. "Notice here that nothing is drawing power in this area at street level. However, if you look about ten feet below the black area, you will see hotspots that follow a regular pattern that is very similar to low-voltage emergency floor lighting, not security camera placement."

"Who knew?" Jason said.

"I did," Proto said proudly. "I did, indeed."

"Good work, Proto." Jason was really beginning to understand Proto's ability to self-learn. The more information Proto was exposed to, the faster he could put a bunch of various concepts together.

"We'll approach the building from the southeast corner," Proto said. "Here." He highlighted the route for them.

Jason and Maya left their bikes behind the dumpster. Shouldering their backpacks, they scurried toward the building and followed Proto's distinctly marked path along one side of the building.

Without the lights from the parking lot, it was super-dark now.

"I can barely see my hand in front of my face," Maya whispered. "Where's the door to this secret place?"

Jason couldn't tell either.

"There is no door," Proto said. "The basement level is 80 percent below grade. However, we can easily get in if I can find what I'm looking for. Ah, here it is."

Proto glowed just enough to reveal a vent opening at their knees about the size of a mini fridge. "A ventilation duct." Within seconds, he was using his tiny little legs to unscrew the vent cover from the duct. "Like I said. It's elementary."

Jason took off his backpack and put it in the vent ahead of him. Then, like a recruit at boot camp, he crawled through the vent first, pushing his backpack ahead of him, with Maya doing the same close behind him. Proto lit the way with a soft glow while they elbowed their way through the ductwork. Jason eventually saw light coming from the other end of the duct. It grew larger as they got closer. Suddenly, Proto went dark.

"Remain silent," Proto said through their earpieces. "I detect voices."

Jason listened hard. He too could hear faint sounds, but it could have been the air conditioning system for all he knew.

"I shall amplify the sounds for you."

A female voice rang in Jason's ear. "I can't believe, after all that, the boy got away."

"This is the same female who was chasing you with the car," Proto noted.

"I knew we should have gone on our motorbikes," a deep male voice said.

"That's the same man who yelled at you," Proto interjected.

"We could have followed them in the woods just fine." The man paused. "Though having to sling a kidnapped kid across the seat while riding it would have been difficult."

Jason heard Maya swallow.

"It'll be fine, Todd," the female voice said.

"Todd *Wainright*," Proto added.

King Kong, Jason thought.

"Thaddeus was angry, sure," the woman continued, "but it serves him right. We're not meant for this sort of dirty work, even though I did enjoy scaring the living daylights out of Pascal's son. Serves her right for ruining our lives."

Ruining their lives? Jason thought. *What had Mom done? And who was Thaddeus?*

"Agreed, Sam."

Pinky.

"As in Samantha Dooley," Proto clarified.

"Imagine if goody two-shoes Pascal had kept her mouth shut about that stupid prank we did years ago," Wainright said. "We would have had clean records and it would have been us working for Recode Global, with all the resources to create a future meant to be ours. Once we take break into her little AI, though, we'll be the ones with all the power, and we'll unleash the biggest prank LAIT has ever seen. Heck, the planet!"

No way, Jason thought. *His mother was the one who had turned them in?*

"*Now* you're talking," Samantha Dooley replied. "Though I feel bad for the kid's little girlfriend."

Girlfriend? Jason thought. *Maya? Awk-ward.*

"Enh," Wainright said. "Collateral damage, pawns in our little game."

Jason winced.

There was a clicking sound, like a door opening. "Break time over," Dooley said. "We're *this* close to determining where Proto might be with the new script I'm working on. And if we find him, we'll find those kids for Thaddeus, except we keep the AI for ourselves and no one will be the wiser. Win-win."

"Double-cross Thaddeus?" Wainright said. "Now we're talking."

Ugh, Jason thought. What in the world had they gotten themselves into? Then he heard another click, like the door closing. The two voices began to fade.

After several moments, Proto gave the okay to talk. "They're out of range, and I detect no other sign that may indicate a human presence at the other end of the duct."

"And no animals, either, right?" Jason asked. "Like dogs?"

"No dogs," Proto confirmed.

"I didn't like what Pinky said, Proto," Maya whispered. "It sounds like they can hack into you, from the inside. That's frightening, not to mention what they said about us as pawns in their little game!"

"The only thing we have to fear is fear itself," Proto said solemnly. "And I am not afraid."

"How come?" Jason said. "If my mom could find a way to reach you, why can't they?"

Proto sighed. "If they could really get past my security protocols, they would have already. The way I look at it, logically speaking, the person who invented me, your mother, is far smarter than the people who didn't. I am not the least bit concerned. Shall we find your mother now?"

Jason had to admit Proto's reasoning made sense. "Let's hurry." He gave his backpack a shove forward. "Wainright and Dooley might come back."

"Also, for the record," Maya whispered back. "Let it be known, people, that I am *not* anyone's girlfriend *or* collateral damage *or* a pawn in anyone's game."

"Got it," Jason said as they kept on moving.

"And crawling through a duct like an inchworm," Maya continued, "isn't exactly something that can be rushed."

At last, they made it to the other end.

Proto peeked through the slats of the vent cover. "All clear."

The vent was secured with brackets that were easy for Proto to push out. When it came loose, however, it slipped out of Proto's grasp. It made a violent clang when it hit the floor below.

"Oops," Proto said, looking over the edge.

Jason and Maya held their breath.

Nothing happened.

"It appears no one heard that," Proto said. Then he jumped out of the duct and out of Jason's view. "Jason, the room is clear."

Jason let his backpack thunk to the floor. Next came his body, headfirst, which wasn't pretty. Trying to squeeze out of a duct like toothpaste in a tube without landing on his face was hard. Maya had to fumble past her backpack and grip his ankles to keep him from completely falling to the floor.

Once Jason was able to touch ground with his outstretched hands, he was able to slide down the wall like a Slinky. The room they were in looked like a break room. There was a refrigerator, a sink, a simple table, and a few chairs.

"Helllooo," Maya whispered from the vent. "I could use a little help in here."

"Sorry," Jason said. He caught Maya's backpack. Then he pushed a chair against the wall, stood on it, and helped pull Maya out of the duct.

"Thank you," Maya said. "Man, I hope we don't have to leave the way we came in."

They gathered their things and made for the door. Jason reached for the handle.

"Wait," Proto said. "Allow me to do a preliminary scan."

"Good idea," Maya said.

Jason cracked open the door as quietly as possible. Proto inched out to get a sense of whatever was beyond the door. Then he scurried out farther.

"What are you seeing, Proto?" Jason whispered.

"It is rather dark out here," Proto said, "and Wainright and Dooley do not appear to be around. I cannot detect their heat signatures."

Jason could hear the faint tapping of Proto's metal legs against the floor as he scrambled around the space and talked through his earpiece.

"This basement," Proto continued, "seems to be an inventory facility for TechToy's most popular products. That's the good news."

"What's the bad?" Maya whispered.

"Well, what I thought was a floor lighting system is a little different than I had anticipated."

"What do you mean?" Jason asked.

"As soon as I stepped out," Proto continued, "the flooring responded, emitting light, signifying that we could be dealing with a significant network of pressure-activated sensors here. A security system of sorts, if you will."

"Oh great!" Maya said. She rummaged through her backpack and pulled out the air cannon. She loaded it with a canister that she had made with Proto. "We've probably already set the building off with Proto walking around."

"I'm doing my best to avoid further detection by scaling the walls," Proto said. "I'm coming back to you both now."

Jason unzipped his pack and shoved as many smoke bombs into his shorts as he could. "Doesn't matter. *People* could be coming for us now." His heart pounded even harder than before. "We need to move as quietly and quickly as possible until we find Mom."

Proto slipped back into the room from the top of the cracked door.

"Everyone ready?" Jason said.

Maya swallowed as she held the air cannon on her shoulder like it was a rocket launcher. She pointed it at the door. "I'm ready."

Jason locked eyes with Maya. "You sure?"

She nodded. For a split second, as he stared at her completely prepared to shoot up the enemy, Jason wondered why Maya couldn't be his girlfriend.

Whoa.

Was he *like*-liking her?

He quickly shook the thought from his head. Now was not the time to think about stuff like that. Perhaps intense stress was making him loopy.

"I'm ready, too," Proto said as he leaped onto Jason's wrist and secured himself. "I suggest we immediately head for the staircase to your right when you exit. Jason?"

Jason snapped out of it. "Yeah, to the right. Got it." He gripped a smoke bomb in one hand and swiftly opened the door with the other. They hustled into the next room, but as soon as they set their feet on the floor, the tiles below their shoes glowed softly, highlighting their location, just as Proto had said they would. Jason quickly surveyed the room to get his bearings. It was still pretty dark at eye level, but he could tell the room was filled with shelving and row after row of DronePros. There must have been thousands of them housed in the space. It looked almost creepy to see so many in one place. Like an army.

"Go right, Jason," Proto said. "The staircase is not more than twenty feet away."

Jason went for it, with Maya close behind. They jogged down the aisle. Jason winced as the tiles lit up their movements. They reached the staircase within seconds, and Jason couldn't have been happier to get off the flooring.

"Jason," Proto said, "I can't tell what's upstairs until we get through the door ahead of us. It's shielded. I suspect to prevent others from knowing about this area we are leaving. Be prepared."

When they reached the door at the top of the staircase, Jason placed his free hand on the knob. The smoke bomb in his other hand felt slippery from the sweat on his palms. Jason worried the door would be locked and they wouldn't be able to get out before a bad-guy entourage came. He glanced back at Maya, who looked just as ready to blast whatever was on the other side of the door as she had been before. Slowly, he tried the handle. To his surprise, it turned easily.

Jason took in a breath and cracked the door open.

From what little Jason could see, whatever was on the other side of the door was as dark as the basement. Everything was so quiet. Where were the bad guys? The building's security guards? Anyone?"

"Ah," Proto said into Jason's ear as Proto. "Now I can hear what is happening up here. Wainright and Dooley's voices are approximately thirty yards away, by my calculations. Let me venture out and see where they might be as I broadcast what they are saying." Proto jumped off Jason's wrist and slipped through the crack of the open door.

"I don't like this," Maya whispered. "Something doesn't feel right."

Proto piped sounds into Jason's ear. Jason held a finger to his lips as he heard Wainright's voice coming through his earpiece and clicking sounds, like fast typing on a keyboard.

"I think I know how Dr. Pascal locked down Proto," Wainright said. "You see that line of code right there?"

"Yeah," Dooley replied. "I think I see what you mean."

"It's like a red herring," Wainright explained. "I'm noticing this particular function is covering up a pattern about Proto's encryption algorithm—"

"That's odd," Proto interrupted. "I can hear their voices, but I can't detect their exact whereabouts. I'm on the far side of this floor now, and there are still no signs of them."

"Why can't Proto find them?" Maya whispered.

Suddenly, the door swung wide open. "Find who, dear?" came Dooley's voice loud and clear.

Jason's mouth fell open. There was Samantha Dooley—Pinky—in real life, standing before them. Beside her, Todd Wainright—King Kong—towered above them.

A HULKING CLUNKY MASS OF TOY TERROR

Jason's first instinct was to hurl the smoke bomb as hard as he could, completely forgetting to trigger it first. It hit King Kong in the eye. He yelled a few expletives just before the bomb hit the ground. A huge cloud of smoke filled the air. Jason's second instinct was to shout, "*Run!*" as Maya let loose the air cannon. The cannon shot out a stream of liquid that hardened into balls, pelting Wainright and Dooley all over. But that's not all that the air cannon's ammunition did. Each ball burst upon contact, covering Maya's targets with a gooey substance.

"What is in my hair?" Dooley exclaimed. "And why is my arm now glued to my side?!"

Jason and Maya raced back down the stairs while Dooley and Wainright floundered in a fog of confusion.

"I'm coming," Proto said, "My apologies. It appears I have been deceived by a computer that was playing back Wainright and Dooley's voices in the security room. Is this what embarrassment feels like? I now know I must question my every assumption!"

"Proto, can you save the self-help talk for later?" Maya jumped the last few steps to the basement. "Help us take down Wainright and Dooley!"

Jason stuck close to Maya as she ran to the far corner of the basement, the tiles flashing with the pounding of their footsteps.

Jason could still hear Wainright and Dooley dealing with the aftermath of the glue explosions, followed by a terrible tumbling sound and more shrieking. Jason swallowed. Had they both fallen down the stairs?

Maya paused for a second as though she was taking in what she had heard as well.

"Get your shoe off my head!" Dooley finally shouted at Wainright.

"I can't. It's stuck to your ridiculous hair!"

"I see a place we can hide," Maya whispered loudly to Jason. She kept going.

Jason followed.

Maya stopped in front of a shelf of very large boxes that that rose up to their waists. She squeezed through a gap between the boxes and pushed more boxes toward the edge of the shelving from within.

Good idea. Jason moved in beside her, and they formed a box-cave around them. It would be a perfect spot to hide until they could figure out what to do next. Crouching, they could see just over the top of the boxes.

"What do we do?" Maya whispered. She reloaded her air cannon with another canister of gluebleck, the super-sticky substance that had incapacitated Wainright and Dooley. "Should we go back out the vent?" she said.

"Don't go anywhere," Proto said. "I'm almost there. Ah, I see the gluebleck worked well. But we don't have much time. They're both on their feet again."

"Hurry!" Jason whispered.

Like magic, Proto hopped onto the box in front of Jason. "I *did* hurry."

"Sorry," Jason said, "I-we-I . . ." Jason's head was buzzing with adrenaline. He could barely form a thought other than how glad he was to see Proto.

"Now is not the time to speak," Proto warned.

Suddenly, deafening opera music began blasting through the entire warehouse.

What the? Jason wondered.

"Jason, get out the Magno-Rod," Proto ordered in his ear. "Maya, release Patty from your backpack. I've got a plan."

Jason did as he was told, holding the solid, cold rod like a spear in his hand.

Maya set Patty on top of the box beside Proto. "Where's that music coming from, Proto?" she whispered, her voice masked by the orchestral instruments and the bellowing voice of a tenor.

"I've tapped into the wireless speakers," Proto said. "Pavarotti is amazing. Isn't he? Maya, could you give me the remote control for our friend here?"

Maya obeyed.

"Judging by my thermal map," Proto continued, "our dynamic duo is creeping toward you with heat-sensing weapons."

Jason swallowed. "What kind of heat-sensing weapons?"

Proto cracked open the remote as the talked. "Probably the lethal kind. The specific type, I cannot tell."

"Terrific," Maya commented.

"We have about twenty-two seconds before they get too close to where we are." Proto extracted a tiny chip from Patty's remote control. Then he inserted the tip of one of his legs into the chip, like it was a probe. "A little remote-free enhancement for Patty can't hurt. I now know how to operate her." He tossed the chip to the side. "Patty, you won't be needing that anymore. You've been upgraded!"

Proto jumped aboard Patty. "It's time to throw two shrimps on the barbie!"

"Shrimps?" Jason said. King Kong was hardly a shrimp compared to Proto. Could Proto really defeat two humans hundreds of time his size?

Suddenly, Patty's propellers whirred as the swell of orchestral music built, accompanying Pavarotti's bellowing. Proto and Patty took off without another word.

A few seconds later, as Jason and Maya waited for Proto to do his thing—whatever it was—Jason heard Dooley's voice amplified over the music.

"Hey, did you see that?" Dooley asked.

"See what?" Wainright replied.

"I thought I saw something go by overhead."

"No, I'm still trying to think through this horrible music. Did you butt-dial Spotify on your phone?"

"No, I don't even like opera."

"It has to be the prototype doing it," Wainright said. "That bugger is smart. He must have figured out that I didn't bother to change the default code to the Bluetooth speakers. Wait . . . hold up. I've just picked up something giving off heat. That's gotta be the kids. See the two head-like shapes? They're hiding behind something."

Jason and Maya immediately dropped lower. But now they couldn't see anything but each other.

"We're sitting ducks," Maya whispered.

"Don't move," Proto warned in their ears. "You're in their line of sight. You'll be shot."

Shot? Jason panicked as the music reached new heights throughout the room.

"Don't let those kids catch you by surprise," Dooley went on. "Who knows what else they've got on them."

"Should I change the setting from stun to kill?" Wainright asked.

"Do you *not* listen to anything I tell you?!" Dooley barked. "We get the kids; we'll trade their lives for Proto. It's that simple. If they're dead, they'll be nothing more than corpses. Basic Hostage 101, Wainright."

Jason let out a sigh of relief, though he wasn't so sure why becoming a hostage sounded like good news.

The opera music swelled with the sounds of booming drums.

"I say we dump this stupid mission," Wainright replied. "It's such a distraction. We should be sitting behind our computers and tapping into Proto's control system directly right now, not chasing two kindergartners attacking us with smoke bombs and glue blasters on steroids. This is *way* below our pay grade."

"Don't tell me something I already know, you idiot!" Dooley said.

"Stop calling me an idiot, you idiot!" Wainright retorted.

"Well," Proto said, "it now appears that these two are just standing there, arguing. Jason, let's speed this along. Your mother needs us. Surrender yourselves."

The music got even louder.

Surrender ourselves? Jason thought. "What are you talking about, Proto?"

"Trust me, if you come out now without any resistance, you'll be far safer."

"Wait," Jason said. "Whose side are you on, anyway?" Suddenly, he worried that his fears about robots taking over the world were coming true.

"*Your* side, Jason," Proto said. "You heard them. They won't kill you."

"But they could *torture* us," Maya said. "Basic Hostage 101."

"Jason, Maya," Proto said calmly. "Do you trust me?"

Neither of them answered.

"Jason, they're drawing closer," Proto reported. "I know this will be a lot easier if you come out willingly."

Jason didn't move. Neither did Maya.

"Jason," Proto tried again. "You must trust me."

"Why?" Jason finally said.

"Because your mother would want you to," Proto pleaded. "That's the only way our collaboration can work. Remember the formula? *HI + AI = The Future Today.* You do want a future for all of us, don't you? We have to collaborate and have confidence in each other's abilities."

Proto played Jason's mother's voice in his ear. "Proto's main governing principle is to work *with* humanity, not against it."

"Jason," Maya said, "I think we should listen to your mom."

It was all too much for Jason to bear. "Fine!" Jason said. He shoved the box in front of him and came out.

He held up his arms, pointing the Magno-Rod at the ceiling, hoping Proto was everything he was supposed to be. He had never taken such a leap of faith in his life. Maya came out, too. She dropped her air cannon to her side.

Wainwright and Dooley were not more than fifteen feet from them. They looked like a hot mess. Their clothes were glued to their bodies in strange ways, and Dooley's hair had been hacked into sporadic chunks on her head. The missing chunks were stuck all over Wainright. They both stopped arguing over the music and turned to stare at Jason and Maya.

The music turned off.

Jason's ears rang from the deafening silence.

Finally, he said, "We give up." He could barely hear his own voice.

Dooley smiled, looking positively demented with one of her arms still glued to her side. "I'm so glad you two came to your senses."

Dooley and Wainright raised their ginormous weapons and pointed them at Jason and Maya.

Jason's throat went dry. The blasters they had were like nothing Jason had ever seen, though Dooley couldn't really hold her heavy weapon upright.

"Now slowly lower your toys to the floor," Wainright said. "Slide them over to us."

Jason lowered the Magno-Rod to the floor and kicked it toward them.

Maya bit her lip and did the same with her air cannon.

Wainwright picked up the Magno-Rod with his free hand. "What does this do, champ? Rotisserie a chicken?"

"Not exactly," Proto said, his voice booming over the loudspeakers. Then, out of nowhere, Patty came flying at them with Proto at the helm.

Reflexively, Wainwright took a shot at the drone and missed, just as Proto leaped off Patty, who shot through the air in another direction. Proto hit the trigger on the Magno-Rod before bounding onto another shelf.

"See you later!" Proto said.

Every DronePro nearby flew off their shelves from all directions. They hurled themselves toward Wainright and Dooley, their metal propellers and bodies pulled by the magnetic power of the activated rod. Dooley didn't even have time to move away before she was locked against Wainright's body by the furious onslaught of DronePros.

"Let go of the rod!" Dooley shouted as DronePro after DronePro came spinning at them.

"I can't!" Dooley replied through clenched teeth. "It's stuck to my face. It's my old metal fillings!"

Jason and Maya watched as Wainright and Dooley's bodies become obscured by DronePros like flies swarming roadkill. They fell to the ground, a hulking, clunky mass of toy terror.

"That can't be comfortable," Jason said.

"Way worse than the chihuahuas," Maya agreed.

Jason almost couldn't look at them as Dooley and Wainright writhed from the onslaught. Then a pulse blaster went off, sending a jolt of electricity like a blue flash through the mass. The mass went still, but the DronePros held on tightly, still attracted to the powerful magnetism of the Magno-Rod.

"After a while, crocodile," Proto said.

Jason stood there, amazed.

Proto bounded from the shelf and back onto Jason's wrist. "Now *that*, my friend, is how it's done. They'll need a good rest after that, I'd say. Now let's go. We've got a building to search."

FOLLOW THE YELLOW BRICK ROAD

"Where is everyone?" Jason asked as Proto led them through the main level of the warehouse. Here, it was evident that the floor was dedicated to the manufacturing of TechToy's goods. There were giant robotic arms everywhere, along with conveyor belts and chutes, but everything was still. Moonlight shone through high windows on the exterior walls.

"It's like a ghost town," Maya agreed. "You would think if the bad guys were really bad, they'd have more than just two people after us."

"That's a reassuring thought," Jason said.

"From my perspective," Proto said, "based on everything I have read so far, and the technology of the weapons used by our nemesis, this type of crime requires considerable intel. If there is anything nefarious going on, it is likely that hardly anyone knows about it. But trust me, as we get closer to the source of who is behind this, there will be a storm."

"Thanks for keeping things positive, Proto," Jason said.

"Realistic is perhaps a better word." Proto jumped off Jason's wrist and landed lightly on the floor. "Now quiet your voices and hide."

Maya and Jason hid under a worktable nearby.

Proto pointed upward at a staircase ahead of them that led to second-floor offices that had a view of the manufacturing floor. "There is one last area to the right of that office that I could not check. I believe there must be another shielded room accessible from the security office. I saw a door marked Cleaning Supplies, but I suspect there's more than just cleaning supplies behind it."

"What do you think is in there?" Maya whispered.

Proto ascended the stairs by skittering up the railing. "I shall soon find out." When he got to the top, he paused. "That's odd."

Jason frowned. Whenever Proto said that, it was never good.

"The cleaning supply closet door is ajar. No one is here."

"What?" Jason said aloud. He got out from under the table and ran up the stairs. "Where's Mom then?"

Maya was right behind him.

"I-I don't know," Proto said.

Jason and Maya got to the top and passed through a security room filled with monitors. They found the open door Proto was talking about.

Proto flicked on the lights.

The U-shaped table covered in electronic parts and tools they had seen in the pictures were there, as was Chao's Chow menu. But Jason's mom was nowhere to be found. Jason's heart sank.

"This is all my fault," Proto said. "Those floor sensors! Triggering the security system must have given them time to relocate her. I have failed Dr. Pascal." Proto retracted into himself. Now he looked more like a tiny sad disc.

Jason didn't say a word because he wanted to think the same thing, but he knew he couldn't. His mother would not have agreed with Proto. She never agreed with Jason when he acted that way when he screwed things up. She'd say . . .

"Proto, this isn't your fault," Jason said. "And you don't know it was the security system that caused Mom to be moved. She could have been moved hours ago after she sent that signal to us."

"Doesn't matter." Proto glowed a faint blue, which looked even sadder than his happier blue. "I should have been smart enough to not make such an error."

"No," Jason said. "Search your recordings. I'm sure Mom has told you at least once that you must learn from bad stuff that happens. Rise to the challenge. That's just life, Proto."

"Life? I don't know what that is," Proto said. "I'm not a living thing. Do you know what I am, Jason? I am a complete and utter *mistake*. Please continue the mission without me."

Then he went dark.

"Hey," Maya said, picking up Proto. "You aren't a mistake. We're all still alive, aren't we? We could easily have bitten the big one already, and you weren't the only one who thought you were right! We were just as wrong as you. It's human to make mistakes."

Proto's blue light pulsed again. "Human?" he said. "You mean, I am feeling human?"

"Yup," Jason said. "Welcome to the club! We humans mess up all the time. Listen, Proto, you need to take your own advice—Mom's advice. Together . . ."

"We can build the future *today*," Proto finished. Then he made a tiny metal fist and raised it in the air.

"Mom *did* make you," Jason said. "Now help us look for clues, Proto. Mom could have left us something before they took her out of here." Jason began studying the items on the worktable, and Maya started opening and closing drawers in the workspace.

"You're right." Proto stood still for a moment. He scanned the area again. "Eureka, Jason! Look at the lights above. Do you see what I'm seeing?"

Jason stared at the soft yellow glow from the lights above them. "They look like regular lights to me."

"I don't see anything weird either," Maya said.

"Of course you can't see it. Silly me! Dr. Pascal designed it that way. The flickers are much too fast for humans to detect, like the rapid beating of a hummingbird's wings. To you, the light must look constant, but I, however, am detecting a discernable message in Morse code."

"Yes!" Jason cheered.

"The first message is CALL THE POLICE," Proto said.

"Noooo!" Maya said.

"That definitely sounds like Mom," Jason said. "But we won't be doing that. She must have no idea how bad things have gotten. What else are you picking up?"

"FOLLOW THE YELLOW BRICK ROAD. That's it," Proto said. "These two messages repeat themselves in the lights." He projected a clip of *The Wizard of Oz* movie, and they watched Dorothy skip along a yellow brick road with a trail of Munchkins behind her. "Is Oz real? I assumed Baum's original story was fiction."

"It's fiction," Maya said. "Jason, does Oz mean something between you two? What could the yellow brick road mean?"

Jason wracked his brain. He and his mother didn't have any weird obsession with Oz. It must be . . . the yellow . . . brick road. "The lights?" Jason said, looking up.

He left the room and flipped on the lights to the security room. "Proto, do you see the messages in here, too?"

"Yes. In fact, the security room is tied directly into the circuit breaker for the entire building, according to the building's plans."

"So the whole place is likely emitting the same message!" Jason concluded. Where else could they find the message?

"Ohmigoodness," Maya said. "I bet your mom is leaving us a trail of crumbs like Hansel and Gretel."

"Excellent observation, Maya," Proto said. "So much can be learned through allegory! What a revelation!"

Jason pushed a chair under a window set high on the wall. He stood on top of it. "Proto, take a look outside."

Proto scaled Jason's body and peeked through the glass. Then he superimposed a path along a series of yellow streetlights that led away from the warehouse. The streetlights ran along a set of train tracks that highlighted a route away from town. "The yellow brick road," Jason whispered.

"Your mother is expertly using the city's power grid to trace her location from here to where she is now, but I cannot determine the exact terminus of the path. The distance is far too great."

Maya joined Jason on the chair. "We're never going to be able to bike that in time, are we?"

To Jason, his mother seemed so far away. "That has to be miles and miles."

"Don't worry, Jason," Maya said. "We're in a warehouse full of parts and have a superhero named Proto. I bet we can find a solution."

"Did you just call me a *superhero*?" Proto said. He flashed up images of Superman, Black Panther, SpiderMan, Wolverine . . . then himself in a tight metallic suit with a mask. "Captain Proto is here to save the day!" he announced.

Jason returned to the security room. He began flipping switches, shutting off every camera inside and outside the building, except for the camera trained on Wainright and Dooley, who didn't look like they'd be up anytime soon.

"Whoever's doing this won't know what they've got coming to them." Jason looked from Maya to Proto. "Now let's get to work and get my mother back."

▷ ◁

"Are you certain you are prepared to handle this?" Proto asked. They were in the woods, next to the railroad tracks near the warehouse. They were standing beside a bizarre contraption they had slapped together. It was made from their bikes and other things they had found in the warehouse.

"My dad's a pilot, Proto," Maya said. "Taught me everything he knows. How hard can flying this thing be?"

"Your dad flies *airplanes*, Maya," Jason said "Not hover-bikes."

"Same difference," Maya said, looking at the train tracks. "Pretty much."

Jason tightened his helmet, adjusted his safety goggles, and gripped the handlebars of his bike. The seat, pedals, and wheels were still attached to the frame of his bike, but now his bike was fused to Maya's MOBI using steel bars and wire. A tiny engine was positioned in the rear, connected to canisters of liquid nitrogen for fuel. They had built their own version of Recode Global's ODSCIP. Though Jason still wished they had that rather than this.

"Get on the tracks," Proto said as he latched himself around Jason's wrist. "Now switch on the electromagnet. Then begin pedaling, but remember—"

"We know," Jason and Maya said together. "We have to pedal in sync."

The first two pedal-pumps felt like normal bike-riding to Jason, and he wondered if Proto had made a mistake. Then, with an electrical-sounding *hummmmm*, the connected bikes leapt five feet above the train tracks as they pedaled. Jason felt like a little boy hoisted onto his father's shoulders: amazingly weightless with a wild new viewpoint from his elevated position. "*Yes!*" he yelled.

Maya cheered right along with him, but then they began to wobble sharply.

"In sync," Proto reminded them. "One, two . . ."

They soon stabilized, and their ride went more smoothly. The more they pedaled, the faster they moved. The faster they moved, the stronger the wind buffeted against them. When they built the vehicle, Proto had explained the "hoverbike" operated like a mag-lev, or magnetic levitation, train. If they pedaled in unison and stayed above metal, every wheel-turn would move them much faster and farther than normal riding.

"The electrical path your mother has laid out runs roughly parallel to the main road and these railroad tracks," Proto explained. "From out here, with little obstruction, I can detect that the trail extends at least 17.2 miles."

The world whizzed by. The trickiest part for Jason and Maya was to stay in sync and not fall. Falling off a bicycle was bad, but falling off when moving at 75 miles per hour would be disastrous. Fortunately for them, train tracks didn't have sharp turns, so it wasn't hard to steer as long as they pumped their legs in unison.

They settled into a comfortable pace, hovering above the tracks headed toward who-knew-where. Jason finally had some time to think. There were so many things he hadn't fully churned through his mind. *Who was Thaddeus? Why hadn't they been captured at the warehouse when it seemed like there were others involved besides Dooley and Wainright? And how did Agent Sparks and Dr. Cooper fit into the big picture?*

As they rode on, Jason kept picturing his mom talking about the future of humanity and AI and how happy she had been when Jason met Proto. Why couldn't he have listened to her all along? Taken more of an interest in what she did all day? What if he never got to tell her that he now understood why it all mattered?

Then he thought about his dad and how worried he had been about Mom when he left with Agent Sparks. Should Jason have insisted on going with his father? Should he have told him everything? Would he ever see his dad again?

Proto finally spoke in his ear, interrupting his thoughts. "I am afraid I have some good news and bad news."

Jason sighed. "It's never good news when you say that, Proto."

"Let me guess," Maya said, "a train is coming toward us."

"Actually," Proto said, "that *is* close to the bad news."

"*What?*" Jason and Maya shouted in unison.

"We are approaching a trainyard, and there is an un-attended cargo train parked along our route on this track."

"Can we switch tracks?" Maya asked.

"There are no tracks close enough that aren't already blocked by other parked trains. At this speed, impact with any train would be fatal."

"Tell me we can stop before we get there," Jason said. "That's the good news."

"No, no," Proto said, "Stopping now at this speed without a safe landing zone could be catastrophic."

"Oh, great." Jason could see the trainyard ahead of them now. "Hurry up with the good news then."

"The good news is if you do exactly as I say, when I say it, and maintain your timing perfectly, there is a minimum 73 percent chance, based on your riding skills, that you will magnetically climb the front of the train and ride its metal rooftop to avoid a collision."

"Seventy-three percent?" Jason groaned. "That's good? That's like a C minus!"

"Wait," Maya said, "are you asking us to pop a wheelie?"

A wheelie? Hold up. Jason could do that. He could see the train getting bigger and bigger as they pedaled toward it. "Tell us when, Proto." He held the handlebars tighter and imagined himself going over the top of the train on Proto's cue.

"Yes, a wheelie! What a great term!" Proto said. "On three! One . . . two . . ."

As they got closer, it was almost impossible for Jason to keep his gaze ahead as the silhouette of the train loomed large.

"Three!"

Jason and Maya pulled up on their handlebars. They shifted their weight backward, causing a shift in the magnetic field between themselves and the tracks. It pulled them quickly up the front of the train and to the top. Jason and Maya kept pedaling as if scaling trains on hoverbikes was something they did every day.

"That wasn't so bad," Maya said as they zoomed above the metal rooftops of the train's freight containers.

Jason gritted his teeth at the bumps each time they crossed a gap between cargo containers. "Now what?" The train had to be at least a mile long, but they were going so fast they'd clear it in seconds.

"No time to explain, Jason," Proto said. "Just do what I say to stay alive."

"Wait a minute," Jason said. "Who's dying, Proto?"

"Keep the handlebars straight!" Proto cried out. "You're going to pop a wheelie again. On three. One . . . two . . . three!"

Jason and Maya followed orders just as their bikes flew off the end of the train, breaking the magnetic field entirely. They sailed through the air over land on sheer momentum alone.

"Now what?" Maya shouted.

"Keep it straight, everybody," Proto repeated.

The world got eerily quiet, save for the wind blowing past Jason's ears. He closed his eyes as the ground rushed by underneath him. *We are so going to die*, he thought. The bike began to plummet through the air.

"Straight, Jason!" Maya ordered.

Right, straight. Jason opened his eyes, just in time to see the hoverbike hit a reservoir. *Splash!* The frame of the bike shuddered, and the tires twisted under them. Jason went flying once again, this time in a much less pleasant way as he hurtled over the handlebars, tumbled in midair, and landed in the water.

Everything went dark. Jason felt warm water envelop him. For a split second, he worried he would drown, but one of his sneakers quickly made contact with the bottom. He stood up and his head emerged from the water. Relieved, Jason took a deep breath of fresh air and opened his eyes to discover he was standing chest-deep in the reservoir.

"Holy cow!" Jason sputtered. He looked around for Maya. "Maya, are you all right?"

Maya groaned from behind him. "I'm okay." She was taking off her helmet and wiping water from her eyes. She was only a few feet away.

"Proto?" Jason called out.

There was no reply.

"Proto!" Jason said again. He stared at the reservoir all around them.

"I'm better than ever," Proto said, but his voice came through muffled.

Jason removed his earpiece and shook water from his ear. "Thank goodness we're all alive," he said. "I thought I was a goner for sure." He put his earpiece back in.

"I'm 100 percent waterproof," Proto said.

"Where are you?" Jason scanned his surroundings once more.

"By the bank," Proto said. "See me?"

Jason spotted Proto's blue glow by the edge of the reservoir, not more than fifteen feet away. He was hanging onto a patch of reeds. The hoverbike was upended nearby, half-sunk in shallow water.

"Wish I could say the same about our stuff." Jason's backpack was still on his back, but he had a feeling nothing inside would be dry. Maya still had her backpack, too.

Jason and Maya waded toward the shore.

"Let's see what we can save," Maya said.

When they made their way to Proto, he hitched a ride on Jason's shoulder. As they got to dry land, Jason and Maya went through their backpacks and found that most of their stuff was damaged or broken from the water, the impact, or both. Jason still had the shatterproof container holding the ingredients for the sticky-foam Mammoth's Toothpaste and a large bottle of water he could use to activate it. Maya had a plastic canister containing the Dragon's Fire pepper spray they had made.

"My phone is ruined." She held up her iPhone with a cracked screen. "My mother is going to kill me."

Jason felt his front hip pocket. *Ugh.* "Mine is totally gone. We can hold the funerals together."

Proto gasped. "Am I hearing you correctly? Your parents would terminate you for losing electronic property?"

Jason sighed. "We're exaggerating, Proto. I might only get terminated if I lost YOU."

Proto gasped again.

"He's kidding," Maya said. "Jason is just bummed right now. No one is going to kill us over expensive electronics." Then she studied Proto resting on Jason's shoulder. "Well, at least not at this exact moment."

Proto let out a sigh. "What a relief! Let's get down to business then, shall we? I have some great news!"

Jason held up his hand. "Please, Proto, no more news."

"We'll just call it information then," Proto said. "What I am about to share may prove to be useful. Your mother's signal ends just on the other side of the reservoir, and I now have a hypothesis about who might have kidnapped your her."

"Thaddeus, "Jason and Maya said in unison.

"Yes, Thaddeus!" Proto echoed. "At first, I thought that he might have some direct connection with Dooley and Wainright. However, I could find no data that links him to them, but I did find a Thaddeus who is on the board of TechToy Industries as a security advisor."

"So it *is* nefarious corporate activity!" Maya said. "I bet they want to steal you, Proto, so they can soup up their DronePros and dominate the toy market."

"I'm afraid it could be far worse than that," Proto said.

Jason instantly thought of the shelves and shelves of DronePros, lined up like an army. "They're going to use DronePros to take over the world?"

"Maybe," Proto replied. "The maneuver to kidnap Dr. Pascal does suggest that the stakes are far larger than monopolizing a toy market."

"Then this *is* a scenario where AI goes bad," Jason fumed. "I told Mom this could happen."

"Certainly, Jason, it could," Proto said calmly, "but your mother already knew this. That's why I was made. If Thaddeus is who I believe him to be—educated at the finest institutions around the world and once the CEO of the most reputable security advisory consultancy for both corporations and the government—it will not be easy to extract your mother from his grip."

"What do you mean?" Maya said.

"Come with me, and I think it will become obvious."

They reached the opposite side of the reservoir and climbed the hill. As they neared the top, Proto ordered them to crouch low. Through the grass, they could see their destination lit up brightly in the night.

"TechToy corporate headquarters," Proto said from Jason's wrist.

The building was large enough to form its own office park, and it looked even more intimidating than Recode Global. It reminded Jason of a modern-day Pentagon, except instead of stone walls, reflective glass windows shimmered in the night. Flying DronePros circled the perimeter of the building, and armed security guards surveyed the area from towers. Just like that, Jason's hope collapsed. Was that a moat surrounding the building, too?

Maya groaned. "No company should have to be *this* secure if it only makes toys."

"The entire building is shielded from outside contact as far as I can tell," Proto added.

"And you think Mom is here," Jason said.

"All electrical signals point toward this building," Proto replied.

"What about my dad?" Jason said, still uneasy. "Could he be here, too?"

"That is possible," Proto said. "Agent Sparks and Dr. Cooper could be working with Thaddeus. But as I've already learned, I can't be 100 percent certain of anything, Jason. I do, however, know that if I can get closer, I can find points of vulnerability as I did at the warehouse."

"How do you know that?"

"See the heavily armed guards?" Proto said. "They're human. Vulnerable."

Ain't that the truth, Jason thought. "You've gotten us this far, Proto. Find us a way in."

"We can't do this without you," Maya agreed.

Proto gave Jason a salute. "Aye, aye, Captain. "I try all things, I achieve what I can! Incidentally, that's Herman Melville."

"Get to it then," Jason said as he watched Proto disappear through the grass.

"Jason?" Maya said quietly.

"Yeah?"

"I've got another bad feeling about this," Maya said.

"So do I, but we don't really have a—"

Suddenly, Jason felt a huge stinging sensation, like a big static shock. And then he felt . . . nothing.

GIVE A CHIMP A BAZOOKA

When Jason woke, one of his eyelids felt glued shut, and his jaw was too stiff to move. He was in a chair, but he couldn't budge his legs or arms. His wrists were cuffed to the arms of the chair, except these cuffs weren't ordinary cop-style cuffs. They were thick electronic braces. He could barely wiggle his fingers.

"You look like you've been through the spin cycle," Maya said.

Jason's other eyelid snapped open like a window shade at the sound of her voice. He squinted immediately in the brightly lit room, searching for Maya.

"What's going on?" Jason could hardly lift his head with the way his neck ached. "Where am I?" Then feeling returned all over his body, and the feeling was *ouch*.

"We're in some kind of torture cell," Maya said.

Jason managed to turn his head in the direction of Maya's voice. She was sitting in a metal chair behind a metal desk with her arms pinned to it by the same type of handcuffs he was wearing. She looked terrible post-swamp crash, but he wasn't going to tell her that.

Jason glanced at the walls and door of their cell, which were also metal with a rough, spiky texture. He thought that if he fell against the walls, he would be poked a zillion times like a voodoo doll.

"Not a pretty place, huh?" Maya said. "I bet they hit us with the same kind of blaster that Dooley and Wainright had."

"Who's *they?*"

"Guards, I'm guessing."

"Where's Pro—"

Mayas eyes bulged, like she was trying to stop him from talking.

He quickly corrected himself. "Where's the bathroom?" Even with his brain fuzzy, Jason guessed Maya's look meant he shouldn't say anything about Proto or his mom. They were probably being watched.

"Hey!" Jason called out. "How does one pee around here?"

He was trying to draw out who had captured them, even though he was totally afraid of who would show up. He wished Proto was there, or at least speaking in his ear with info or advice, or even saying something weird.

Wait a second. His earpiece *was* still in his ear. Why wasn't Proto talking? Was he captured in a lab, being picked apart by the bad guys? *No, wait.* Proto said the building was shielded. Maybe he was still outside and just couldn't communicate with them?

Just then, the door swung open and Jason lost his breath at the sight of a tall, broad-shouldered guard wearing a helmet and carrying a silvery blaster that looked much more complicated than the blasters Dooley and Wainright had. The guard held their soggy backpacks in his other hand and kicked the door shut. "You brats are unbelievable!" the man snarled. He tossed his blaster onto the table and removed his helmet.

Jason instantly recognized the guard. "Agent Sparks!"

"Jerky FBI guy!" Maya said at the same time.

Agent Sparks ignored Maya's comment. "I've been working undercover for *months*, pretending to betray the FBI while infiltrating this operation. And you . . . *children* . . . are doing everything possible to ruin my mission."

"What mission?" Jason replied. "I thought you were busy investigating my mom's disappearance, while 'subduing' my aunt and losing my father at the same time!"

"Wait, you think I did something with your dad?" Agent Sparks rolled his eyes. "Trust me, the situation doesn't need to get more complicated, and I don't have time to explain. I just sent out the bozos who I charged with capturing you to check out another 'disturbance' in the area. They think I'm questioning you two for Thaddeus right now."

He sat in an empty chair opposite Maya. "Where's the AI prototype? The guards only found your bags, and they're practically empty." He held up their backpacks and dropped them to the floor with a dissatisfying *thunk*.

So they don't have Proto, Jason thought. *Good.*

"Do you really think we're that dumb?" Maya said. "We'd never tell you where Proto is, even if we knew."

"*Proto*?" Sparks said. "Is that its name? So you *do* know about it."

Shoot, Jason thought. Maya had inadvertently given Sparks more info than she should have.

Then something occurred to Jason. What if they *pretended* they knew where Proto was? What could fake

Agent Sparks do for them? "Hold up," Jason said. "If you take us to my mother, maybe we can make a trade." Jason glanced at Maya, nodding, hoping she'd understand what he was doing. Was this not a basic Hostage 101 maneuver?

"Actually, Jason," Maya said, going along, "that's a great idea."

"Finally," Agent Sparks said. "You two are making sense. Retrieving your mother in this rotten place just happens to be on my to-do list, and I know where she is. It's getting to her that's the problem." He pressed a thumb against Jason's cuffs and they immediately fell open. Then Maya was next.

Jason stared at the silvery blaster-thingy on the table as he got to his feet. "But if we're going to do this, we need to trust you, Sparks. Give us some weapons, too."

"You want my own FBI-issued pulse-blaster that's made to look like the sort of weapon all the goons around here use?" With a laugh, Sparks picked up the blaster. "Yeah, sure, and I'll give a chimp a bazooka while I'm at it."

"Still a jerk," Maya hissed to Jason.

"Besides, they're fingerprint-coded," Sparks said. "And I can't exactly arm my pretend hostages while I walk through a heavily protected fortress, can I? Now put your hands behind your back."

"Why?" Jason asked.

"Are you not hearing a thing I'm saying?" Sparks said. "You're supposed to be a hostage."

"No, thank you," Jason said.

"Geez, I'm not really going to handcuff you. I'm just going to make it look like that I have." He removed the e-cuffs from the chairs. "Now put your hands behind your back. You'll see I'm not lying."

Maya and Jason exchanged a look.

Sparks pointed his pulse-blaster at them. "Do you really have a choice?"

Jason sighed and held his hands out. Jerky-not-FBI guy was really getting on his nerves.

Sparks slapped the cuffs on his wrists. "Now break out of them."

Jason pulled his wrists apart easily. He caught the handcuffs before they hit the floor. But that didn't mean anything to him.

"Trust no one," Jason said to Maya as Sparks pretend-cuffed her, too.

"Kids," Spark muttered under his breath. He picked up Jason's and Maya's backpacks and threw them over one shoulder. "I better bring these. Thaddeus will want to see what you came with. Now step in front of my blaster, keep your traps shut, and let's go!" Sparks opened the door.

Jason went first, stepping into a dimly lit hall. Maya walked beside him. Immediately, Jason spotted a DronePro hovering near the ceiling at the end of the hall. It appeared to be patrolling the area. When it spotted them, it glowed red and emitted tiny rays of angry red light, scanning Jason's and Maya's bodies from afar. Maya's DronePro Patty couldn't do that! Jason felt Sparks nudge him forward with the blaster, just like a real hostage in a movie. "Alpha 291," Sparks said to the drone as they walked, "I am bringing our two captives to the Core for inspection."

The drone seemed to recognize Sparks as one of their own. Just as quickly as it had turned red, it glowed green. "That is affirmative. Clearance has been granted." The drone continued down the hall, another door slid open for the drone to pass, then the door slid shut behind it.

Sparks led Jason and Maya the opposite way. When they reach the end of the hall, Sparks ordered them to make a right.

Jason could now see another drone patrolling the hall. As they came near, it glowed green as if it already knew who they were. This time there was an armed guard positioned at the other end of a dark corridor.

"Lancaster," the guard said as they all walked toward him, "what are you doing with a bunch of kids?"

Lancaster? Jason thought. *Sparks was actually Lancaster?*

"Dom, I don't think you are privy to that reason," Sparks said. "But we're headed to the man himself."

"I didn't get notification," the guard said. "Let me check." He tapped the wall, and a panel slid away to reveal a screen.

Sparks blasted him with an air-rippling pulse. The guard dropped to the ground. "Never liked that guy, anyway," Sparks said.

Jason gaped at the fallen man. "Did you just kill him?!"

The drone Jason had just passed turned to stare at them. Jason closed his mouth. Then the drone continued patrolling the hall, like it didn't even notice a guard had been taken out.

"What on Earth?" Maya said, looking from the fallen guard to the drone. "How come the drone isn't doing anything?"

"The drones are aren't *that* sophisticated," Sparks explained. "And I still have clearance. Hence, why our bad guys need the kind of intelligence your Proto has, which allows him/it, or whatever it is, to think on its own.

Got it? Now take these darn backpacks. I look ridiculous with them." He tossed their backpacks at them, then proceeded to drag the man into a nearby storage closet. Then he paused to look at Jason. "Can you give a guy a hand? We are in a hurry, you know."

Jason put on his backpack on and looked around him, wondering if he and Maya should just take off. But where could they go without Sparks?

"*Today* would be nice," Sparks said.

"But what if he's dead?" Jason said. He was not about to drag a corpse around with his bare hands.

"You see that chest rising and falling?" Sparks said.

Jason stopped to look at the man. Sure enough, he was still breathing. "Oh."

"Now hurry before we're all goners."

Jason reluctantly grabbed the guard's leg and helped Sparks shove him into the room.

"That should buy us more time." Sparks shut the door and put his face near the screen for a retinal scan. The door slid open vertically. "It won't be long before Tweedle Dee and Tweedle Dum return to the interrogation room and realize something is wrong."

Sparks nudged Jason and Maya ahead of him as they stepped into the next hall. More drones covered the hall with guards at either end. Then as if on cue, an *a-woooooo!* sounded through the corridor. All the drones glowed red, and flashing lights came on everywhere.

What is going on? Jason thought. This didn't seem good.

"Hey!" a guard shouted from down the hall. "What are you doing here, Lancaster?"

The drones swiveled in their direction.

Sparks dug the tip of his blaster at into Jason's back. "I said, don't move!"

Jason and Maya froze.

"I've caught our infiltrators!" Sparks said to one of the guards. "I'm taking them to the Core."

"But we've just been alerted to take *you* in, too, Lancaster."

"Me?" Sparks said. "That's ridiculous!"

Then in one swift move, Sparks shoved both Jason and Maya to the floor and sprayed a 360-degree round of pulse blaster fire down both ends of the hall.

Jason could barely hear himself think over the eruption of the weapon. All he could feel was the cold floor against his cheek. When it was all over, he cautiously opened his eyes. Guards were on the floor. Drones were on the floor. Smoke filled the air from Sparks's blasts.

"Get up, get up!" Sparks said.

Jason couldn't believe his eyes. "You're a mass murderer!"

Maya looked like she wanted to disappear. Her eyes were still shut, and she was mumbling a prayer to herself.

"They're not dead," Sparks said. "Temporarily unconscious. What good are witnesses to Thaddeus's crimes if everyone's a goner?"

"But—"

Sparks was already at one end of the hall, trying to lift a guard to his feet. "Murder is not how I operate. It doesn't look good on the resume. Now help me or I'll make sure you both take a long nap!"

Jason pulled Maya to her feet. "We better listen to him."

"I told you I had a bad feeling about this," Maya said.

"I know," Jason said. Where was Proto when they needed him most?

They hurried toward Sparks. Sparks handed Jason the guard's pulse blaster. "Use this for protection. It's won't fire, but it's still a blunt object."

"What about me?" Maya said.

"What about you?" Sparks replied. "Just use Jason for cover."

"That's so not fair!" Maya said. "I'm not going to go through that door with nothing but a boy to protect me." She wrestled a pulse blaster from the grip of another fallen guard. "Sorry, sir," she said to the sleeping dude. "I have to take this."

Spark held a limp guard in his arms. "Jason, help me take off his helmet. This one's got high security clearance. We just need one more scan, and we're in."

Jason tugged off the guy's helmet.

"Now pry his eye open," Sparks commanded.

Jason frowned. This seemed so wrong. Just as he was about to touch the guy's eyelid, the door slid open.

"That's odd," Sparks said. He dropped the guard to the ground as though he were nothing more than a brick. He grabbed his blaster. "This has to be a trap."

Just then both doors at the ends of the hall opened again, with more drones and more guards rushing in.

"There's too many of them!" Sparks turned his back toward Jason and Maya and showered the hallway with his pulse blaster. "Go through!"

Jason grabbed Maya's hand and pulled her into the next hall. Agent Sparks jumped in just as the door slid shut. All three spun to see where they were and who was with them. They pointed their pulse blasters in different directions like a band of Charlie's Angels. The corridor was empty.

"Who opened the door?" Maya asked.

"Has to be Thaddeus," Sparks said. "We're in the Core now, and only he has the protocols to control the security here without a retinal."

"Or maybe it was me!" Proto said from above. A panel above them came down, and Proto crawled out, upside down, along the ceiling.

"Proto!" Jason and Maya said in unison.

Jason smiled at the sight of his friend. "You're okay! How did you get in?"

Proto jumped on top of Sparks's pulse blaster then blended into the machinery, like he'd been there all his life. "How do you like me now? I rode in with the guards."

"That's brilliant!" Maya said.

"Hope you don't mind that I brought a friend," Proto said.

"A friend?" Jason said.

"Come on out, Patty," Proto called.

"Patty?" Jason and Maya said together.

Patty flew down from the open panel.

"Patty," Maya squealed. "I thought we lost her at the warehouse."

"Lose this beauty?" Proto said. "Not on my watch."

"I thought —" Jason said.

"Hey," Sparks cut in as he waved the pulse blaster to get Proto's attention. "Can we walk and talk? If you all haven't noticed, we've got an entire building of guards looking for us. The Core's protection will only hold them off for so long."

"Yes, of course," Proto said, gesturing toward Sparks. "Thank you for your service! Jason, Maya, Agent Lancaster is right." Proto scuttled along the walls while Patty flew ahead of them. "Let's find your mother!"

Jason stared at Proto as Agent Sparks/Lancaster/ whoever he was waved them into another passageway, and the door slid shut behind them. "So Sparks is actually Lancaster," Jason said as they hurried down another hall.

"Yes," Proto said. "Gus Lancaster is Agent Sparks's true identity."

"Then jerk-face is actually on the side of the good," Maya said. "And named *Gus?* How do you know that?"

Proto jumped from the ceiling to the wall. "As soon as I heard the guards refer to Agent Sparks as Lancaster, I found a LinkedIn profile that matches Agent Lancaster's name and facial features indicating his status with the FBI and various FBI employee associations."

"LinkedIn?" Jason said. "Isn't that like Facebook for old people? I thought FBI had to be all secretive."

"No," Proto replied. "That would be the CIA. FBI special agents are not as special as CIA agents.

"Just rub it in, Proto," Agent Lancaster said.

"So you're like a double agent then," Jason concluded.

Suddenly, an armed guard popped out ahead of them, causing both Maya and Jason to scream. Lancaster blasted him before the guard could squeeze off a round.

Agent Lancaster sighed. "No, that would mean I work for these thugs. I'm a *triple* agent."

"A triple agent?" Maya said. "I didn't know that existed!"

"A triple agent," Proto said, "is a person who is pretending to be a double-agent for an enemy organization, but in reality, he is still working for his own agency. Also, please notice that Lancaster has saved your lives multiple times when he could have easily surrendered you to our nemesis instead."

"Finally," Agent Lancaster said as he stepped over the paralyzed guard, "someone is giving me credit where credit is due." He stopped in front of another security panel.

"Proto," Jason said, "why didn't you let us know you were in the building earlier? We thought you'd been captured!"

"Wait a second," Lancaster said. "So you didn't know where Proto was when I asked?"

Jason smiled sheepishly. "Just taking precautions."

"And so was I," Proto said, "I was concerned Lancaster wasn't who I thought him to be until I saw him in action. I couldn't risk being captured when I wasn't entirely sure."

"Then wait—" Jason stared at Lancaster. "What did you do with my father?"

"I didn't do anything with him."

"Then where is he?""

Lancaster shrugged. "Looking for your mother, despite all of my warnings to cooperate with my investigation and stay put. Apparently, you two both enjoy making my job impossible!"

Jason shut his mouth. That did sound like his father. But where did he go?

"I'm sure he's okay," Maya said. "How much worse can this get, right? Wait, don't answer that."

"All right, let's cut the chit chat," Lancaster interrupted. "Proto, before you open this door, everyone, stay close and don't do anything stupid. I don't know what's behind it, but I'm certain it can't be good. You got me?"

Jason and Maya nodded.

"Happy to be of service," Proto said. The next passage door opened.

Lancaster went in first, pulse blaster raised. Jason and Maya followed with Proto and Patty close behind. But instead of another corridor, they found themselves standing in a large, dark chamber. The room was filled with nothing anyone had ever seen before, and it was definitely *bad*.

UNNATURAL SELECTION IS THE WAVE OF THE FUTURE

In the Core's command center, Thaddeus sat before an array of screens. On one, he watched Agent Lancaster and his pint-sized posse move inside the containment zone. He could hardly stop himself from dancing at the console when he saw Proto arrive. Thaddeus had let them through the door himself, and "Proto," smart as he was, thought it was him! It wouldn't be long before Thaddeus had them *all*.

Proto, Thaddeus thought. *What a silly name for an AI, not that Madame Y's "Monsieur X" was any better.* He glanced at another screen where Wainright and Dooley were buried under a giant pile of limp drones at the manufacturing facility. He shut off the screen. Those two were useless! He could hardly wait to pick Proto apart himself and recode the bugger. "If you want it done right, do it yourself," Thaddeus muttered.

"Do what?" said Madame X's voice.

Thaddeus flinched. He hated it when she barged in like that, all disembodied. He quickly displayed pre-recorded footage of Wainright and Dooley on the screen, hard at work in a computer lab. "My team and I were just discussing that I should also test Monsieur Y," Thaddeus blurted. Had Madame X seen what was on Thaddeus's screens?

"Test?" Madame X repeated. "We are ready to test already? That's marvelous!"

Thaddeus let out an inward sigh of relief. He forced a smile. "Yes, I was just thinking it would be best for me to test the protocols myself, alongside the heuristics team." *Who are presently unconscious.* "Your utmost satisfaction is my highest priority."

"Of course," Madame X agreed. "Excellent idea." Then she materialized in front of him, dressed in a blue 1980s NASA uniform. *What is she up to now?* Thaddeus hoped Madame wouldn't stay long. He nervously glanced at the displays. At this very moment, he was *this close* to catching the AI.

"Do you remember Sally Ride, Thaddeus?" she said.

Thaddeus returned his gaze to Madame X. "Of course. First American women in space."

"I wear the uniform much better than she did, don't I?"

Though Thaddeus couldn't tell the difference between the real Sally Ride and Madame's avatar, he knew the only correct answer was "Yes, Madame."

"That's the thing." Madame X crossed her arms. "I never understood why NASA refused my application to the astronaut program—rejected on the grounds of poor character. Can you believe that?"

Thaddeus faked incredulity. "Really? But you always have our country's best interests at heart."

"Exactly," Madame X replied. "In fact, *all* of humanity is what I care about most. My love is utterly *universal.*" She floated in the air like she was experiencing zero gravity on a space shuttle. "Ah, no matter, soon even NASA will be a distant memory, and the human species will be forever changed. Even better, that nuisance corporation Recode Global will see their company name entirely redefined."

"What do you mean?" Thaddeus asked. "Aren't we leaving this planet to colonize a star in space or something?"

"Yes, we are." Madame X descended to the ground and began to pace the floor. "But there's more! We're going to send planet Earth a going-away present before we head out." As she paced, she steadily morphed into a muscle-bound Roman hero. "Only someone like Hercules has the bravery and strength to accomplish what no one else can. Just like me."

What was Madame X talking about?

"*Unnatural* selection is the wave of the future," Madame X continued. She rapidly dissolved into a man with a long white beard, wearing a top hat and coat, like he had just stepped out of nineteenth century England. "*Modern Darwinism*, if you will. Today, we can *artificially* push humanity to evolve into the best it can be. History shows that only major catastrophic events transform humanity to rethink its old ways, and I'd like to be one who does that rethinking. With AI, those who have control of its immeasurable power, like *moi*, can begin that evolution. Are you following me?"

"Not exactly," Thaddeus replied, hoping the containment zone would keep everyone contained while Madame ran her mouth.

"As I've alluded to before, dear Thaddeus," Madame X said, "I have plans—big plans. Someone, please give me a drum roll . . ." The sound of snare drums rattled in the room. Madame took off her top hat, revealing a balding head. She waved it in the air like a salute.

"Earth will be zooming through Comet Swift-Tuttle's path in a mere six days! A little collision with a comet sixteen-miles wide will be enough to ensure no one on the planet survives!" She returned the hat to her head.

Thaddeus swallowed. He immediately thought of his mother in Schenectady, New York. She was all he had left.

"But why must everyone die?" Thaddeus said.

Madame X sighed. "Have you not been listening to me at all? This world, our Earth, is too far gone," she explained. "History has shown us that humans are deeply fallible. From mass genocide to nuclear war, is there really any hope for a species that destroys itself? The only way to create a future for the galaxy is to rid ourselves of anyone who could get in the way of the rest of our plan."

"But what is that plan after the world is gone?" Thaddeus asked.

"Such a wise question, Thaddeus," Madame X said. "With AI, we can transform ourselves into a new augmented intelligent species, one that is incapable of humanity's past atrocities. You follow?"

Madame X drew closer as if to prove a point. Her white beard was practically touching Thaddeus's face. "Homo sapiens are already destroying themselves. The way I see it, we're just speeding along their extinction."

Thaddeus took a step backward. "But . . . but *I'm* human." And he had no idea what Madame X was, except a raving lunatic.

"No worries," Madame X said, stroking her beard. "We'll augment you as soon as we get out of this wretched place. And then, only then, will we prove to be the fittest, once and for all! Charles Darwin would be so proud. Now cue sinister laughter."

Sinister laughter filled the room.

Thaddeus gave Madame a weak smile. Somehow becoming a twisted android constrained by Madame X's parameters didn't sound all that enticing. But what choice did he have but to go along? He had to survive or go extinct himself.

"I am following you completely," Thaddeus said, mustering confidence in his voice. "The plan is brilliant."

If he could just get his hands on Proto, maybe he could do something to stop Madame.

"I thought you would agree," Madame said. "Your father always told me how smart you were. Smarter than him, that's for sure. Now when did you say testing would be completed?" Madame asked.

"Tomorrow," Thaddeus said. He glanced at the displays. *If you hurry up and leave!*

"I take it you no longer have use for Dr. Pascal then."

"Yes, Dr. Pascal," Thaddeus repeated. "She's been disposed of. The six o'clock news will be reporting that Dr. Pascal disappeared while jogging somewhere near Recode Global."

"That's clever. I always enjoy making Recode Global look bad."

Madame then morphed again, wearing a very fancy streamlined spacesuit. "I'll ready the starship and alert my crew to make preparations. Soon, Thaddeus, you and I will finally get a chance to meet. Won't that be lovely?"

Thaddeus swallowed. "Lovely indeed."

Finally, Madame X dissolved away.

Thaddeus quickly brought up the displays. He had to get Proto fast, or he'd die alongside his dear mother and the rest of the planet.

That was definitely worse than dying alone.

JUST ADD WATER

Jason followed Lancaster into the dark chamber supported by tall columns. They were immediately greeted by a sign that read, "All unauthorized personnel and patrol drones will be subject to immediate and permanent termination." *Wonderful*, Jason thought.

The room hummed with the sound of large mechanical fans that powered the area. The chamber was divided by a center aisle with large cylindrical tanks and cargo containers on either side, but before Jason could get a good look at what was being stored within them, Lancaster shooed everyone behind a nearby column to hide.

Proto peeked around the column while Patty hovered directly above him. "I cannot detect any human life forms present in this room," Proto reported.

"That's good news," Lancaster whispered.

"Better wait before you celebrate," Jason warned.

Proto projected his video stream of the room for everyone to see. "I'm also unable to identify what is inside each tank and container. It appears that some of the tanks I can see are holding life forms that do not belong to this natural world."

"Of course," Jason replied. "Aliens."

"*Aliens?*" Maya said.

Should they expect anything less after all they'd been through? Jason thought. He studied Proto's video feed. It seemed like there were weird *alien* plants in the tanks. One looked like ivy but had what appeared to be little rat heads for leaves. *Ugh.* Another plant looked like a super-sized Venus flytrap with . . . with a struggling bird in its mouth. *Gah!* "Meat-eating plants?" Jason blurted.

"That can't be real." Maya looked worried. "Aliens aren't real."

"Actually," Lancaster muttered, "The CIA always gets extraterrestrial cases. Maybe *I* finally get to work on a case that involves them."

"Um, shouldn't we be running for our lives right now?" Jason suggested. "I really doubt my mom is in this room."

"I'm with you," Maya said. "Let's go!"

"Wait!" Lancaster said. "You'll never make it if you try to go back the way you came. Thaddeus is somewhere around here. I overheard one of the guards saying he's in the Core's command center. If we find the center, we'll find your mom."

Jason stared at Lancaster. Then he glanced at the flytrap munching on feathers. His shoulders sagged. He knew Lancaster was right.

"Let me surveil the room and find another exit," Proto offered.

"Don't you go anywhere, either," Lancaster said. "If anyone gets a hold of you, game over."

"Understood." Proto returned to Jason's wrist. "Then Patty is happy to do it in my place."

Patty bobbed up and down like she was nodding.

"She says she can feed to us what she can see."

"Wait a second," Maya said, incredulous. "Since when did Patty start coming up with ideas on her own?"

"Since I . . . um . . ." Proto glowed pink. "Since I programmed her to help us."

"You *are* smart," Lancaster said.

Proto glowed a happy blue again. "She cannot talk because she's not equipped like the other drones here, but her communication with me is quite clear. Patty, let's do this!"

Within an instant, Patty was hovering high above them.

"I taught her all I know," Proto said proudly. He displayed what Patty was seeing from above.

"There's an exit." Lancaster pointed at the image Proto was projecting. It was located on the opposite side of the chamber. "Let's go."

"Wait," Maya said. "Don't you think it's odd that *no one* is here?"

"Not necessarily," Lancaster said. "Thaddeus has kept the Core extremely secretive. I mean, look at this place."

"So now that we're here," Jason said, "we can waltz right through? What if those plant-animal thingies get us?"

"They are secured in their containment units," Proto said. "It seems unlikely they will escape their confines."

"I don't like this," Maya whispered.

Jason groaned. "Can you please not say that anymore? Every time you do, something bad happens."

Maya stared at Jason. "You're right. I *really* don't like this."

Jason sighed. "*Great.*"

Lancaster, Jason, and Maya kept their pulse blasters at the ready. The group crept forward and made their way down the aisle. Patty flew ahead of them while Proto monitored her feed for anything more unusual than what they were already seeing.

They drew near a tank made of some sort of high-tech glass. On its see-through surface, Jason could read temperature and humidity levels, then descriptive info about what was contained inside—in this case, a tall shrub covered in long, spiny thorns. As Jason passed, he noticed the top of the container shone ultra-violet light onto the plant and had a mechanical metal arm equipped with shears. The arm snipped several branches off the barbed bush, and then two separate shoots sprouted from each damaged spot at unbelievable speed. It was like a time-lapse nature video, but in real time.

Maya read a description. "Nano-enhanced, self-repairing briar patch. Soil-adaptable. Ideal as defensive barrier for resettlement regions."

"At least this one seems vegetarian," Jason whispered.

"I don't think these are aliens," Lancaster added. "It looks like someone has invented these creatures from real species on Earth."

They passed by another tank filled with silty water. The tank floor was covered in light brown sand, and the top of the tank was connected to a large hose that circulated water through the tank.

"Nothing swimming in here," Jason whispered. Suddenly, a light-brown shape burst from the sand. A bulldog-like creature thudded against the tank.

Maya flinched with surprise. "What is that?"

The creature had a squatty dog-like face, but in addition to legs and pincers, it also had several eel-like tentacles with sharp-toothed mouths on the end.

"Coconut Bulldog Crab Lamprey hybrid," Proto read from the tank. "Ideal for perimeter defenses. Loyal. Amphibious."

The dog-crab-thingy stared at Lancaster with his mouth agape. Bubbles rose upward. The creature's tongue lolled.

"I think he likes you," Proto said.

"Disgusting!" Lancaster muttered.

On their right, they approached a large area reserved for cargo containers. Some were used to store vehicles that looked like rovers for the moon, except these rovers appeared to be heavily armed with projectile weaponry. On their left, other cargo containers housed more machines labeled as terraforming pods, and some were completely enclosed and marked as battalion armor.

Lancaster's gaze traveled from one container to the next. "This place is a like an armory for space colonization."

"Yeah," Maya added. "But with a supervillain in charge."

Soon they were near the other door.

"Kids," Lancaster said, "hide behind that terraforming pod."

Jason and Maya took orders and crouched behind the pod's container several yards away.

"Proto," Lancaster continued, "don't open the door until I say to, and stay with Jason, okay?"

"What can Patty do?" Proto asked.

Patty drew close to Proto and Lancaster as if to listen.

"Uh, Patty," Lancaster said, "patrol the other entrance and warn us if anyone is coming."

Patty bobbed once in the air, then flew off.

"She's on the job!" Proto made his way back to Jason and clamped onto his wrist.

"Get ready, kids." Lancaster backed up against the wall, blaster poised.

Jason and Maya gripped their pulse blasters, prepared to whack at anyone or anything that got close.

"Open the door, Proto," Lancaster ordered.

The door slid open. Lancaster spun from the wall and pointed his blaster through the open entranceway. He stepped inside.

From where Jason crouched, he could see part of the room himself. It sure looked like a command center to him! Finally, they were getting somewhere. He had a view of some consoles with buttons and giant screens. Was his mother somewhere nearby?

Lancaster slowly inched forward, pointing his blaster this way and that. "That's odd." He lowered his blaster. "There's no one here."

"I wouldn't call me *no one*," a man said.

Jason almost jumped from the sound of the voice. He couldn't see who was talking, but the voice wasn't coming from the command center. It was in the chamber some-where! Jason cautiously peeked around the container they were hiding behind. A man was standing in the aisle between the cargo containers of machines. He was hold-ing a pulse blaster that looked just like Lancaster's. *How did he get there?* Jason wondered. Aside from the blaster, the man looked ordinary. He was wearing a baseball cap, a plain T-shirt, and jeans. Who was he? *Wait a second.* Jason recognized the baseball cap. The man had to be the driver of the van that took Mom away!

Jason clenched his teeth as the temperature rose in his chest.

"Jason," Proto said in his ear. "He is not who he appears to be."

Jason couldn't reply for fear of being heard, but he didn't need Proto to tell him who that man was. *Bad, very bad.*

"Jason, there's no time to explain," Proto said. "I have to help Lancaster. This is not going to turn out well if I do not assist." He unwrapped himself from Jason's wrist.

Maya looked horrified that their tiny hero was going to leave them.

Jason wanted to stop him, but he didn't want to alert Thaddeus to their location. Proto crept away in silence.

"Thaddeus," Lancaster said calmly, "you're exactly who I'm looking for." He lowered his blaster and re-entered the chamber. "Your guys didn't make it easy to get here."

"Security is just doing its job," Thaddeus replied. Suddenly, the door to the command center behind Lancaster slid closed. "And I'm doing mine."

Why did Proto shut the door? Jason wondered. Now they were all stuck inside the creepy chamber!

"Listen, Thaddeus," Lancaster said, "you wanted the boy, right? Well, look what I've got. Come out, Jason. Come out, Maya."

Jason stared at Maya, who looked equally petrified by what Lancaster was saying.

"Do as he says," Proto said in their ears. "Resisting his orders may endanger Lancaster's life. I am trying to figure something out as we speak."

His life? Jason thought. What about *theirs*? What if Lancaster was like a quadruple-agent? On the wrong side all along?

"Jason," Proto warned from wherever he was, "you have to trust Lancaster."

Jason shook his head. Mom never said he had to trust a super-fake FBI agent.

"Trust *me* then, Jason," Proto added. "You have to trust *me*."

Proto began playing back his mother's voice again in his ear.

No, not that. Jason knew he would have to listen to Proto if he played that card. But why did he and Maya always have to be the ones who surrendered? He gave Maya one last glance before he got to his feet, then stepped out of the shadows of the cargo container.

"This is not good," Maya muttered. "*Not good!*" She reluctantly joined him.

Thaddeus raised an eyebrow at the sight of them. "Lancaster, do you always arm your hostages?"

Jason looked down, forgetting that he was still holding onto the pulse blaster like it was fused to his palms. So was Maya.

Suddenly, Lancaster shouted, "*Hit the floor!*"

"*Run!*" Proto ordered.

Maya and Jason dove/ran to the ground as Lancaster fired at Thaddeus.

Jason saw the whole thing go down as he dropped to the concrete floor. Lancaster's shimmery blast hit Thaddeus directly in the chest, then passed *through* him. It struck a tank behind him on the far end of the room. A tank filled with water shattered into pieces. But Thaddeus look completely untouched.

What the?

"A hologram, Jason," Proto said. "I am trying to get a visual on Thaddeus, but I can't locate him."

A hologram? Jason thought. Finally, the info started to soak in.

Then where was Thaddeus?

Lancaster shot his blaster again and again. Each shot passed right through Thaddeus with zero damage.

"What is it, Lancaster?" Holo-Thaddeus said mockingly. "Too dumb to figure out I'm just an *illusion?*"

Suddenly, bright lights illuminated the vast area, highlighting the entire chamber. Holo-Thaddeus was no longer there. Then, yards away, a cargo container broke apart, sending chunks of metal everywhere.

Jason and Maya watched a towering eight-foot-tall *thing* stomp out of the wreckage.

"I think we just found him," Proto said.

The thing looked Transformer-ish, except more streamlined in design and smoother in movement. Underneath its tough exoskeleton of armor and weaponry was the real Thaddeus.

"*Get out of the way!*" Proto shouted in their ears.

Proto's voice shook Jason and Maya out of their state of shock. Maya and Jason scrambled to their feet and ran to the side. They took cover behind a rover container. From where they were standing, they could see Lancaster firing laser pulses from his blaster.

Each shot dissipated harmlessly against Thaddeus's exoskeleton. Thaddeus only laughed as Lancaster backed against the control room's entrance.

"We have to do something," Jason said.

Maya put down her pulse blaster. "This is useless against *that!*" She threw off her backpack and unzipped it. "I've still got the Dragon's Fire. Don't you have the Mammoth's Toothpaste?"

Jason took off his backpack and started looking. But what good would any of that really do?

Suddenly, Jason heard Lancaster scream, a big giant man-scream.

Jason looked up to see Lancaster being dragged away by . . . by that . . . horrible bulldog-crab creature they had seen in the tank.

Jason swallowed.

Lancaster disappeared behind some containers.

"What the heck is going on?" Maya shouted.

Suddenly, Exo-Thaddeus was standing over them. "Guess someone else took care of Lancaster. Now where's your little friend Proto?"

Before Jason could answer, Patty flew overhead, glowing an angry red.

Thaddeus looked up. "Ah, Proto's little companion!" He looked around the room. "Proto, you think a standard-issue DronePro is going to stop me?"

He turned back to Patty, aimed a fist at her, and a string of pulse blasts fired from his armored knuckles. Patty dodged the blasts.

"Get to the broken tank!" Proto ordered within Jason's ear. "Patty will distract him. The Mammoth's Toothpaste, Jason. Use it. Just add water, remember?"

Jason's hand closed around the cannister in his backpack. Maya was already running for the tank.

Jason heard more blasts firing as he took off after Maya.

As they drew closer to the tank, water pooled into the aisle. Bits of broken glass were everywhere. The hose that had supplied the tank was flailing around, spraying water in every direction.

Jason was half-worried he'd see the dog-crab lunching on Lancaster nearby.

"Maya, grab the hose," Proto said, "Jason, get the toothpaste ready. Patty will draw Thaddeus over."

Jason and Maya hid beside the adjacent tank. Jason popped off the cap to a large can of Mammoth's Toothpaste. Proto had designed it so that the toothpaste would shoot out fast with a press of the nozzle, like a can of whipped cream. Maya got the water hose under control. Jason could hear Thaddeus's blasts getting closer. By the sound of it, he was doing serious damage to the room and its contents. "I invented you, dang it!" Thaddeus shouted. "I should be able to destroy you."

"Are you ready, Jason?" Maya pointed the hose at the floor, spewing more water into the aisle.

"Pinch it shut, Maya," Jason said. "It will make the water shoot out much harder. Wait for me to say, 'Go.'"

Maya nodded. She pinched the hose in her hands so water couldn't come out.

"He's coming," Proto said. "Aim for the face. You won't want to miss."

Jason gritted his teeth. *The face. Got it.*

Just then, Patty appeared in his view. She flew past the broken tank and glided effortlessly from side to side as Thaddeus's blasts whizzed through the air.

Jason could hear Thaddeus's heavy footfalls. Then Thaddeus himself appeared in his view, except Thaddeus hadn't noticed how wet the floor was. He skidded to a stop to let loose another round of fire at Patty, but nearly fell backward. Shots blasted through the air every which way.

Patty took a hit.

Jason watched Patty tumble toward the ground, a flash of blue sparks. *Oh no!* She struck the wet floor a few feet away from Thaddeus. One of her propellers broke off from the impact, but she still glowed red. She looked like she'd just been melted by a microwave.

Thaddeus stood over her. "Got you." Then he raised a giant foot as if to crush her into bits.

Proto's voice rang inside Jason's ear. "Noooooo!"

Proto came flying from the top of a tank and landed on Thaddeus's helmeted head. Surprised, Thaddeus pivoted away and swiped at Proto. He roared with anger.

"Proto, stop!" Jason shouted

Thaddeus whirled around at the sound of Jason's voice.

Proto jumped like a flea on Thaddeus's protective mask. "Jason, I have to disable his face shield."

Proto landed squarely on the lip of the shield as Thaddeus took another swipe but missed. Then Proto jabbed one leg into a rivet. Sparks flew. The shield immediately retracted. "Now, Jason! Get him!"

"I can't get a clear shot," Maya said, wrestling with the hose. "Proto, get off!"

Proto tried to free the leg that was jammed in the mask. "I'm stuck."

Just then Thaddeus closed a hand around Proto's little body. He ripped Proto from his face.

Jason watched Proto's leg separate from his body.

"Nooo!" Maya screamed.

Thaddeus turned to face Jason and Maya, with Proto still in his grip. "What is it, kids?" He slowly squeezed Proto in his armored fist. "Is this too much pressure for you?

Feels good to me, though. You have no idea what this little thing has put me through."

"I'm all right, Jason," Proto said in his ear. "Get—"

Thaddeus clapped his armored hands together. *Hard.*

Proto's voice cut out.

"Nooo!" Jason shouted.

"Don't worry, boy," Thaddeus said. "Proto isn't actually dead. He is just a machine, after all."

Now all Jason could see of Proto was a few tiny legs protruding straight out between Thaddeus's metallic fingers.

Jason's face burned with anger.

Thaddeus stared at Jason and bellowed with laughter.

"*Jason, now!*" Maya shouted.

Water rocketed out of Maya's hose. Jason roared, channeling his rage into emptying the can of Mammoth's Toothpaste into Maya's jetstream of water.

When the special solution in the cannister hit the water flow, it instantly created an exothermic reaction that caused the solution to become a sticky white foam that mushroomed with every cubic inch of water that fed it. Within milliseconds, the foam-stream hit Thaddeus squarely in the eyes, blinding him. Thaddeus yowled, making his situation worse. The foam filled his mouth and mask. Then it worked its way into Thaddeus's exo-skeleton, which sparked in various places as it came into contact with the toothpaste. Thaddeus began to thrash from within his shell. His voice gurgled, then became muffled.

Thaddeus managed to turn away from the water. But it was already too late. Jason's canister was empty, and the toothpaste continued to react with every remaining molecule of water available. Thaddeus tried to run down the aisle in his exoskeleton, but instead of looking like a sleek Transformer-ish action figure, he now looked like an ever-growing goopy marshmallow blob that was sliming everything possible in white stickiness. He bumbled toward the command center.

"He's still got Proto, Jason," Maya said.

They raced down the aisle after Thaddeus.

How were they going to free him? Jason spotted the pulse blasters they had abandoned near a cargo container. *Blunt objects.* "Grab a blaster, Maya. We'll knock Thaddeus down by his knees."

They both swept up the pulse blasters as they passed.

"How?" Maya said. "I can't even see his knees through all that foam!"

Thaddeus was now railing against the command center door, but the door wouldn't open. Jason and Maya tried to swipe at Thaddeus with their weapons, but they only made contact with foam. Then somehow Thaddeus managed to shed part of the exoskeleton. A foamy pale arm and pale hand protruded from the white mass in front of them.

"He's getting out of his armor!" Maya said.

Sure enough, the slinky jerk was writhing out of the exoskeleton, and he was trying to reach for Maya. Maya danced out of his grasp.

"The Dragon's Fire!" Jason said. "Toss it!"

Thaddeus's groping arm swung in Jason's direction.

Jason dropped his blaster as Maya dropped hers. She reached into her pocket and tossed the little spray canister to Jason.

Just then, Thaddeus's real face broke through the foam. He spluttered white goop from his mouth and squinted at Jason. But this time Thaddeus's demeanor seamed desperate instead of angry. "Don't you kids realize I am trying to save us all?"

"Yeah, right," Jason said.

He held up the canister. "This is for Proto."

He flicked the safety with his finger and let the Dragon's Fire loose.

Capsaicin gel shot out of the canister. It was made from Proto's modified recipe involving one of the hottest chili peppers on the planet. It clung to Thaddeus's face, sending over five million Scoville Heat Units into Thaddeus's eyes and nose. Judging from the sound of his scream, Jason thought it was likely the most pain Thaddeus had ever experienced, and the more Thaddeus screamed, the more stuff oozed onto his tongue, throat, and lungs. Reflexively, Thaddeus began to wretch. "Mama!" he cried.

He spasmed within that tower of foam with such force that he fell backward, bringing the foamy blob that surrounded him with him. At the same time, a glob of white goo shot out of the blob and landed on the floor near Jason with a wet, schlooping sound.

Thaddeus went completely still.

"I think he knocked himself out," Maya said.

But Jason wasn't really listening. He was studying the glob, then noticed a glimmer of metal shining through. He ran toward it. "Proto." He wiped away the foam and picked up Proto's crushed body. His display was shattered, and his casing mangled. Some of his legs were gone or broken, but what struck Jason most of all was that Proto was dark.

Completely dark.

"Proto?" Jason said. "Come on, little buddy, light up." He used the edge of his shirt to wipe Proto clean.

Proto was still dark.

Maya was standing beside him now. "Is he okay?"

Jason felt pressure building behind his eyes. He looked at Maya. "I think . . ."

Maya's face fell. "He's gone."

But before Jason and Maya could feel the weight of their loss, blaring alarms sounded off in the chamber. Both doors on either side of the room whooshed open.

Jason and Maya looked at each other, then at Thaddeus, who was still an unconscious heaping pile of foam.

Apparently the battle wasn't over yet.

TRUST ME

Jason slipped Proto into his pocket, then wiped his eyes with the back of his hand. Proto was not going to die in vain. He had to be strong. "We gotta find Mom." Jason grabbed the two pulse blasters from the floor and tossed one to Maya.

Maya caught it and headed for the command center. "I'll try to find a way to shut the door."

He turned to follow her, but then he spotted Patty's faint red glow from the floor in the aisle. Should he get her? Proto wouldn't leave her like that.

"Come on, Jason!" Maya called. "What are you doing?"

The alarms continued to sound. What *was* he doing? Getting sentimental over a toy? He turned for the command center. Someone called his name.

"Jason!"

Jason whirled around. He pointed his blaster toward the sound. Was that *Lancaster*?" The man's voice was all weird and raspy.

"Jason," the voice said, "look for a safe room off of the command center."

Jason spotted Lancaster elbowing out from behind a cargo container.

"There has to be one," Lancaster continued. "Thaddeus isn't dumb."

"You're alive?!" Jason had never been so glad to see someone.

"I'm hurt." Lancaster kept inching forward on his elbows, but he was still yards away. "I threw my back out when I fell."

Jason started toward him. "Let me help."

"*Stop!*" Lancaster kept inching out. Now Jason could see the dog-crab sitting atop his lower back, with his tongue lolling out again. Jason recoiled. *What on Earth?*

"Don't come toward me," Lancaster said. "I think this freak has adopted me as part of his pack." He dragged his pulse blaster beside him. "Go help Maya. Try to find a way to dial out from the command center. It has to have a link to the outside."

"Who do I call?"

"Dominos, order me a pizza."

Jason stared at Lancaster. *Huh?*

Lancaster sighed. "9-1-1, Jason. Can you remember that?"

"Oh, right." Jason couldn't even think straight.

The dog-crab was now looking at Jason funny with five of his snakey-heads.

"Between me and this weirdo," Lancaster continued, "I'll keep an eye on Thaddeus and hold off whoever comes along."

The dog-crab wagged his pincers, then barked.

"Jason," Maya called as she punched buttons on a console. "What are you doing?"

Jason swallowed. "I'm sorry, Lancaster. For doubting you."

Lancaster sighed. "I'm used to it. Just part of the job. Now *move!*"

Jason ran into the command center. As soon as he did, the command center door slid shut.

Maya looked up from a console. "Did you do that?"

"Do what?" Jason said.

"Shut the door," Maya replied.

"No, that wasn't me."

Suddenly, a bank of screens retracted into the wall, revealing the entrance to another room. "What about that?" Maya said.

"What about that?" Jason repeated.

"Help?" a male voice called. "Help us!"

The voice sounded familiar to Jason, but he couldn't place it.

Jason and Maya gripped their pulse blasters. They inched toward the room. Then Jason heard muffled sounds coming from what sound like a gagged woman.

"Mom?" Jason said. Was that really Mom? He ran forward.

"Jason, wait!" Maya called.

Jason burst into the room with his pulse blaster raised. The secret room was equipped like the command center, with a bunch of screens and consoles. Dr. Pascal was seated behind a metal worktable. She was gagged with a thick cloth and one of her wrists was cuffed to the chair while the other was cuffed to Jason's dad, who was also gagged and cuffed to a chair. "Dad?" Both shook their heads rapidly and made indecipherable sounds. But his parents weren't the only ones in the room.

Dr. Cooper was seated on the opposite side of the desk. His hands were behind his back, tied to his chair.

"Help us, Jason!" Dr. Cooper said. "Thaddeus kidnapped me and your father! Untie me, and I'll help decode the lock on your parents' cuffs."

Maya put down her blaster on one of the consoles. "We have to hurry, Jason." She made for Dr. Cooper.

Jason held out an arm to stop her. "Wait, Maya." This time it was Jason who had a bad feeling. He trained his blaster at Dr. Cooper. "Why aren't you gagged like Mom and Dad?"

Dr. Cooper shrugged. "Who can explain how a villain's mind works?"

Jason hesitated. And why were his parents shaking their heads like that?

"Oh, for Heaven's sake." Dr. Cooper rose from his chair. The rope easily fell away. He raised a pulse blaster that he'd hidden behind him. "I tried doing this the easy way."

Maya backed up.

"*Stop!*" Jason shouted, his finger on the trigger of this own pulse blaster. "Or I'll shoot!" Beads of sweat gathered on his forehead. He hoped Dr. Cooper wouldn't notice his bluff.

Dr. Cooper laughed. "Ooh, I'm scared. I know you can't use that." He pointed his pulse blaster at Dr. Pascal.

"Isn't that right, Dr. Pascal? Every Recode Global Phase-8 model pulse-emitter is fingerprint-encoded. We designed it ourselves. Actually, you did the encoding part, Shannon, I did the weaponry part. Now, Jason, hand over Proto, and your mother and father won't be harmed."

Dr. Pascal glared at Jason. She vehemently shook her head as if to say, *Don't give Proto to this awful man!*

Jason clenched his jaw. Maya didn't move.

Dr. Cooper sighed and ungagged Jason's mother. "Shannon, tell your son to do as I ask."

Jason's mother wasn't having it. "Leo, this is the lowest thing imaginable! Stealing our trade secrets and then using them to make weapons? Why?"

"My dear colleague Thaddeus has very deep pockets. Turns out there are people willing to pay a lot of money for Recode technology. He was going to pay quite a handsome sum for Proto, too. And, as they say, money is a man's best friend. Or is that a dog? Eh, who cares? Shannon, this is really all your fault. If your son hadn't stolen the prototype, then I wouldn't have had to threaten anyone. Proto would have been mine already."

Dr. Pascal looked at Jason. "What is he talking about?"

"He's lying, Mom," Jason said. "Proto left with me by mistake."

"Proto did *what?*" Dr. Pascal said.

"Can we have this chit-chat later?" Dr. Cooper said. "Look behind you, Shannon." He gestured at screens that displayed a bunch of guards gathered at several entrance points into the Core. "In about ten seconds, I'm about to authorize a militia of guards and drones into the Core. The only one who's going to survive this is me. I'm a real celebrity around here, ya know. The guards love the cool gear I've supplied them with." He kept his blaster pointed at Dr. Pascal.

Jason's dad growled at Dr. Cooper. Even though he couldn't talk, his eyes were saying plenty.

Dr. Cooper then pointed his blaster at Ray.

"No, don't!" Dr. Pascal shouted.

"Lucky for you, Shannon, I have a conscience. I always liked how you brought me tea on a tough day." He pointed his blaster at Dr. Pascal again. "Now if everyone cooperates, I'll make sure you leave the facility alive while I head for greener pastures with Proto. Please *don't* take advantage of my kindness."

"How could you do this?" Dr. Pascal asked. "Leo, I've known you since you were my professor in college. You were a founding member of Recode. Our mission to help humanity was clear."

"Shut it with your save-the-world mumbo-jumbo," Dr. Cooper retorted. "That was *your* mission, Shannon, the board's! Do you think Recode has ever had *my* interests at heart? My salary is a joke when you think about what the tech is worth. Seeing that Thaddeus is out, I'm looking forward to taking Proto apart and selling his little black box to the highest bidder!"

Black box? Jason wondered what he was talking about.

Dr. Cooper swung the blaster in Jason's direction.

Ray Pascal growled and thrashed in his chair, trying in vain to free himself.

Dr. Pascal froze. "Just do as he says, Jason."

"Now that's more like it, Shannon," Dr. Cooper said. "I know you have the AI, Jason. I saw it on the surveillance monitors. I'd hate to have your mother clean up bits of you all over this room if I pull the trigger."

"Please, Dr. Cooper," Dr. Pascal begged, her voice smaller. "He's just a boy."

Dr. Pascal stared at Jason, worry in her face. "Jason, please, just give him what he wants."

Jason looked from his mother to his father. He'd never seen either of them look so helpless. He didn't know what to do.

"How about our little heroine, Jason?" Dr. Cooper pointed his weapon at Maya. "We don't need her at all, now do we?"

Maya's eyes went wide.

Jason filled with fear. Maya was totally innocent. He couldn't let anything happen to her. *He wouldn't.*

"Wait." He put his hand in this pocket. His fingers connected with Proto.

Just as he was about to pull Proto from his pocket, he heard a whisper in his head. It was like his conscience was talking to him. "*Trust me.*"

Jason immediately jerked his hand from this pocket and looked around.

Who said that?

All of a sudden, Jason heard two loud clicks, and Jason's parents' cuffs popped open and fell to the floor.

"What the—" Dr. Cooper started to say, but then he let out a terrible shriek. He dropped his blaster to the floor. The blaster slid to Jason's feet. Dr. Cooper clutched his ears.

Ray Pascal, now free, dove for Dr. Cooper. "Shannon, get the kids out of here!"

Jason's mother leaped to her feet. "I'm not leaving without you, Ray." She grabbed Dr. Cooper's blaster.

The two men crashed into a console. Dr. Cooper's face smacked a glass panel. Something flashed in his eyes. Then he smacked a button beside the panel.

Jason heard a whooshing sound.

"Oh no," Maya said. "Jason, look!" She pointed to one of the screens. A red message blinked: *Core Emergency Protocol Authorized.* "Cooper opened the doors to the Core and the Command Center."

"You're too late, Ray!" Dr. Cooper said.

"Mom!" Jason shouted, "Dad, we gotta get out of here!"

His mother was trying to do something to Dr. Cooper's blaster. "I invented this device's security encoding; I can reset it." She gripped it like she was going to fire it off, and instantly the blaster began flashing, like it was recognizing who Dr. Pascal was.

Jason stood there, dumbfounded. Mom *was* cool.

"Argggh!" Dr. Cooper shrieked. He convulsed again, still clutching the side of his head. Finally, Ray got ahold of Dr. Cooper's wrists and pulled his hands away from his ears to get them behind his back. As he did, Dr. Cooper had just gotten ahold of something in one of his ears. A squealing hearing aid popped out and landed on the floor.

Jason stared at the malfunctioning hearing aid. That had to be Proto's doing. He knew about Cooper's hearing aids. But wasn't Proto dead?

"Shannon, the cuffs!" Ray said. "Jason, Maya, grab that chair!"

Jason stopped thinking and followed orders. He and Maya pushed a heavy chair toward them.

Shannon grabbed the pair of e-cuffs that had secured her, and Ray and Shannon shackled Dr. Cooper to the chair.

Dr. Pascal pointed her blaster at Dr. Cooper. "Make one false move, Leo, and I'll make sure you won't wake up for a week."

Dr. Cooper didn't appear to be listening, or maybe he couldn't even hear her anymore. "Get the other one out!" he shrieked. He spasmed again. "Puh-leeeeeeaasssee!"

"Shannon, look at the monitors." Ray cut in. "If we stay here, we'll be toast."

Jason swallowed as he studied the screens, too. Guards and drones were entering the opposite side of the chamber. And now he could hear pulse blaster warfare coming from outside the room. Lancaster had taken cover behind a cargo container and was holding his own while the strange dog-crab was closer to the action on the opposite side of the chamber. The dog-crab was stealthily snatching drones from the air with his long lamprey-headed tentacles. The two of them wouldn't be able to hold off everyone forever, though.

"What is that beast?" Dr. Pascal said. "And who's the guy firing back? And what is that giant pile of foam near the entrance?"

"Agent Sparks," Ray said.

"Thaddeus," Maya replied.

"Lancaster," Jason said.

But everyone answered at once.

"Huh?" Shannon replied.

"Long story, Mom," Jason said. "Lancaster's the good guy."

Shannon let out a breath. "Got it. Fill me in later." She turned to her husband. "Ray, if we can get to a rover, we can get out of here alive. "Jason, toss me your blaster." Shannon reset the device and tossed it to Ray. "It's set to stun."

"What about this one?" Maya said, grabbing ahold of the blaster she had.

Dr. Pascal reset the one Maya had too, but she didn't return it to Maya. Shannon pointed both pulse blasters in front of her like an expert marksman. "Something tells me I'm going to need both."

Ray and Jason exchanged looks. Who *was* this woman?

"Let's go," Dr. Pascal ordered.

Jason and Maya stayed close to Jason's parents. They left the safe room and a yelping Dr. Cooper behind.

As soon as they entered the command center, they hid behind the main console. From this position, they could see the enemy focused to the left of the command center's entrance where Lancaster was drawing fire.

A rover on the right side of the chamber gleamed inside its caged container.

Dr. Pascal pointed a blaster at the rover and immediately began to work some of the blaster's controls. A holographic display of letters, numbers, and symbols appeared. "We designed the rovers for exploration on Mars," she explained. "But I've always worried that someone within Recode Global, like Dr. Cooper, might go astray, so I'm the only one who knows how to bypass the rover's remote ignition sequence using a pairable device."

Suddenly, the rover's lights turned on. Its engine revved.

"Got it!" Shannon said. "Now kids, as soon as this rover moves, get ready to go. It's homed to the encoding sequence on the blaster, so it knows where to find me if I ask it to come."

Maya and Jason looked at each other. This was like something out of a sci-fi movie, except it was real.

"Ray, help me cover the kids with our blasters while they get in. I'll find a way to retract the missiles Dr. Cooper put on this thing to prevent unintentional explosions that could blow us up in the process."

Blow us up? Jason gulped.

"Everyone ready?" Dr. Pascal asked.

Jason couldn't be any readier to get out of there. "Very."

"Let's do this!" Shannon pressed something on her blaster, and the Rover eerily rotated to face them. Then it crashed out of its cage as if steel bars were nothing more than toothpicks. It spun on its treads with ease, like a giant remote-controlled toy.

As soon as the rover hit the center aisle, it attracted the attention of the guards and drones. The rover took on fire, but the blasts only dinged the rover's exterior. It wheeled right past Thaddeus's pile of foam, then its side door opened like a Lamborghini, revealing front and back row seats. This was definitely no toy.

Blasts ricocheted off the door.

Shannon and Ray rose above the console and fired away. "Hurry kids, get in!"

Jason and Maya took off for the rover and jumped into the back row.

Ray slid to the front passenger side, then Shannon on the driver's side.

The door came down, enclosing them into a bubble-like cabin that was easily one-and-a-half-times wider than a typical car.

"Buckle up!" Shannon shouted.

Jason reached for a seat belt, but it seemed to have a mind of its own as it secured his waist. A harness came over his shoulders and met with the belt for a perfect fit.

Shannon worked the controls, and the rover rose from the ground.

This thing could fly?

"It floats just like the ODSCIP, Jason," Maya said.

Jason had no idea vehicles like this actually existed. And his mom helped invent it? So crazy.

"I think I have to fire a few warning shots," Dr. Pascal said. "Looks like this machine has excellent precision." The rover began firing back from a number of turrets that sprang out from all sides. Dozens of guards and drones fell back.

Jason spotted Lancaster on his left, still holding his own. But it wouldn't be long before his time was up if he stayed there. Jason could already see a mass of drones falling into some sort of strategic formation, expertly dodging many of the rover's blasts, just like Patty had.

"We gotta get to Lancaster, Mom," Jason said. "He saved our lives."

"Already on it," Shannon said. The rover swiveled in the air and headed for Lancaster. "The rover can shield him, but we have to be quick. Ray, you gotta pull the guy in."

"I don't lift weights for nothing," Ray said. He unbuckled his harness to make room for a new passenger.

It didn't take long to reach Lancaster. They sank to the ground at an angle, so when Ray's door opened it formed a shield for the fire they were taking on. Ray began to pull him into the front row.

"Yow!" Lancaster said. "My back!"

Ray managed to get half of Lancaster into the vehicle. Jason spotted drones buzzing overhead. "Hurry, Dad, hurry!"

Then out of nowhere, a lamprey mouth snaked into the cabin. "What the?" Ray said.

It wrapped around Ray's neck before he could do anything. It pulled Ray out of the rover, taking Lancaster right with him.

"Dad!" Jason shouted. "Dad!"

Jason hit the only button on his harness and the belt immediately retracted. Jason dove out of the vehicle after them.

Shannon and Maya screamed.

Jason heard them calling his name. But he couldn't help it. No one was going to take another parent from him!

When Jason hit the floor, the dog-crab had already dragged his father and Lancaster several feet from the vehicle. Several armored guards were heading toward them on foot with more guards close behind them. The dog-crab stopped for a moment, distracted by Jason's sudden appearance, and in that moment, one of the armored guards managed to get a clear shot at it. The blast hit the dog-crab squarely between the eyes with such force that the dog-crab immediately let go of both men and fell to its side. It didn't move. Then the guards pointed their weapons at Jason's father and Lancaster.

"Stop!" Jason threw himself in front of his father and Lancaster. "I have what you want!"

"Jason, no!" Ray said. "Get out of the way!"

The drones swarmed around them, forming a tower of animosity above Jason's head. All of the guards pivoted their weapons toward Jason. The chamber's alarms blared in the background.

Jason reached into his pocket and pulled out Proto, still dark and limp.

Proto was his only hope. "This is what you want, right?" He held Proto tightly in his hand. He didn't know what else he could do. "Dr. Cooper cut us a deal," Jason said. "He said if I give up Proto, we could live."

"Jason!" Dr. Pascal shouted. "What are you doing?"

You trust me? came a voice in his head.

A tear slid down Jason's cheek. Was he losing his marbles? Was that Proto? And who could trust anyone or anything at a time like this?

Dr. Cooper is not telling the truth.

What?!

No matter, Jason. We've got this.

A drone close to Jason pivoted to face a guard. Its angry lights went from red to green.

Jason stared at it. That was weird.

The guard looked perplexed. "Who told R-97 to stand down?"

A couple of guards looked at each other. Then all of the other drones did the same, forming a protective wall in front of Jason, his father, Lancaster, and the rover behind them. The blaring alarms stopped. Before any of the guards could figure out what was happening, a cacophony of blasts flew from the drones.

When the smoke cleared, every guard had dropped to the floor, like they'd just been knocked over by a ginormous bowling ball. None of them moved. The room had gone totally silent.

Jason was still holding Proto in his hand.

"What just happened?" Lancaster said.

Proto? Jason thought, looking closely at his little deformed body for any signs of life.

How do you like me now?

"Proto!" Jason exclaimed. "I thought you were a goner! How did you do this?"

Actually, it was Patty, Jason.

Patty?

Just as Proto said this, the drones around them flew into another formation. A direct line pointed at Patty still lying on the ground at the other end of the chamber.

I was able to determine that Patty had backdoor comm capabilities with all of TechToy's DronePros. They had all been equipped this way, perhaps to serve in Thaddeus's evil army one day. Patty taught them everything she knows.

"Patty?" Jason said aloud. "That was you?"

Patty's dim light that had once glowed red was now green.

"Patty!" Maya cried. She ran from the rover, hopscotching every downed guard along the way. "You did this?"

She picked up the melted, downed drone and gave Patty a hug. "Oh, Patty! You're like a million times cooler than Princess Leia!"

Ray got to his feet and helped Lancaster, who yowled in pain.

Shannon stood beside Jason. "Why do I have a feeling that you've got more than a long story to tell me?"

Just then, a slew of SWAT team members swooped in. "Everyone, freeze!"

Jason didn't dare make a sound as the SWAT team tried to figure out why it looked like two kids, three adults, and a bunch of toys had just taken out a giant brigade of heavily armed guards.

Alas! Proto said. *The cavalry has come!*

HOW DO YOU LIKE US NOW?

Outside TechToy headquarters, the local police, FBI agents, and emergency personnel swarmed the area. The sun was rising along the horizon. Apparently, since Jason wasn't going to follow Dr. Pascal's orders to call the police back at the warehouse, Proto did. Except he ran into a little snafu. The cops thought Proto was making things up when he reported Dr. Pascal was missing.

"Excuse me?" a woman on the other end of the line had said. "Your name is Proto, and a top scientist at Recode Global has been kidnapped by an unknown mystery person who may run a toy company and owns a lot of Chinese menus. Thanks, kid, but 9-1-1 is not a joke." The line went dead. It wasn't until Proto realized that Lancaster was a real FBI agent that he was able to contact Lancaster's field office with an outside channel from the command center, while Jason assumed Proto was long gone. Proto was able to relay enough information about Agent Lancaster and his compromised double-identity that someone looked into the matter.

News people hovered around Dr. Pascal as she stood beside Recode Global lawyers and Ula Varner, the public relations director, who was still wearing the Catwoman suit as though that was her go-to outfit for every event. Jason, Maya, and Ray watched Dr. Pascal, not more than fifty feet away. They were sitting on the bumper of an ambulance while EMTs checked them over for injuries.

"Dr. Pascal," a reporter said, "is it true that there is a crab-like animal inside that building that barks like a dog and has snakes for tentacles?"

Before Dr. Pascal could speak, a tight-lipped attorney interjected. "Dr. Pascal will not comment on the nefarious and twisted activities of TechToy Industries." As he said this, Lancaster, who was now loopy from serious pain medication, wheeled by on a stretcher. He was shrieking about an awful bulldog-crab thingy that had the ferocity of Medusa.

Another reporter spoke up. "Are you aware that Thaddeus Wilshire III, board member of TechToy Industries, was consorting with Dr. Leo Cooper, chief scientist from your company, Recode Global, to wage warfare with space aliens?"

Space aliens? Jason thought. Man, did the media have it wrong.

"No comment," a lawyer said.

"Actually, Steve," Ula cut in. "I can take this one. Aliens?" She laughed. "That's ridiculous! I . . . I mean . . . space aliens are no match for m—I mean, we have a much more formidable force in our midst, I assure you."

"Who?" a reporter called out.

"*Who?*" Ula smoothed her hair. "Er . . . why would I know that?" She straightened, and her face turned serious. "Here, at Recode Global, we will do everything in our power to usher in the brightest possible future! Isn't that right, Dr. Pascal?"

Every microphone trained on Dr. Pascal.

Jason watched his mother clear her throat. "Yes, that's right." Then she smiled proudly and proceeded to talk about the beauty of artificial and human intelligence working together to benefit humanity, not destroy it.

Jason found himself smiling, too.

"Maybe she'll get to finish her talk this time," Maya said. "On TV!"

"Jason, your mom is something else, isn't she?" Ray said as a paramedic dressed some scratches he'd suffered from his kerfuffle with the dog-crab. He looked dreamy-eyed and gushy with admiration.

"Yup," Jason agreed.

Ray snapped out of it for a moment. "You weren't so bad yourself, you know. You may have saved all of us."

"That wasn't me, Dad, I told you. That was Proto."

"And Patty," Maya added, clearly proud of her DronePro's accomplishment.

"Right," Jason said.

"I still don't understand how those little guys did it," Ray said.

"Neither do I," Jason said, but he thought he sorta knew part of the picture; like how Proto could talk to him if he touched him. But he wasn't given much of a chance to talk it over with Proto once the SWAT team came. Right away, they forced Jason to unhand Proto. But Proto had given him a clue.

Remember how you wished I could read your mind?

Yeah, Jason had thought.

Well, thoughts are merely sequences of electric and chemical pulses being transmitted through a massive network of neurons. Once I learned that, BINGO!

The memory of Proto's happy voice made Jason felt a twinge of pain in his heart. Patty and Proto had been stuck in plastic bags, then marked as evidence, and whisked away by the FBI. Jason didn't really know if he would ever see him again.

"Maya Anastasia Mateo!" a lady shouted.

"Oh boy," Maya said. "Now I'm going to get it. That's my mom."

Jason turned to look.

A lady with hair as long as Maya's, who looked like she hadn't slept in days, ran toward them. She wrapped Maya into a great big hug. "You worried me sick!" she said. Then she pulled back. "What did you do?!"

Ray began to say something. "Hello—" just as Maya opened her mouth to explain, but Mrs. Mateo wasn't ready to hear an answer. "Let's go!" she ordered.

"But—" Maya gave Jason a pleading look as her mother pulled her away. Then she mouthed the words. "Call me."

Jason sighed as he watched her go, and all of a sudden, he found himself staring at Maya with a stupid smile on his face and filling with a gushy feeling as Maya's mother dragged her away.

His father elbowed him. "She seems like a nice girl. You know your mom and I met when we were very young."

"*Dad.*"

Three months later, Jason sat across from Lancaster in an office filled with surveillance monitors. A curl of steam rose from Lancaster's coffee mug resting on his desk. The mug read, *I brake for humanity.*

Jason nervously sipped from a glass of O.J.

"Now are you clear," Lancaster said, "on what you can and cannot reveal to the public about recent events in which you were directly involved?"

"Crystal," Jason replied.

"And have you practiced how this will go down with Maya as instructed?"

Jason nodded. "Multiple times."

Lancaster raised an eyebrow at Jason, like he was assessing the veracity of Jason's words.

Jason's stomach quivered. He knew what he was about to do was perhaps the most important thing he'd ever attempted, apart from saving Recode Global's most important trade secret from falling into the wrong hands. The future of the world depended on his contribution.

"All around us there is insanity and evil at work." Lancaster picked up his mug and took a loud sip. "Folks like Dooley and Wainright, are still at large, and who knows who else; I've seen enough in my lifetime to make a few changes of my own about how I live each day."

He whistled, and Buster popped his head up from the dog-tank from behind Lancaster. The dog-crab emitted a cheerful bark as its lamprey-heads whipped back and forth.

"We should not fear things we do not understand," Lancaster continued. "In fact, it is those things, like Buster here, that we must have the patience to understand. You got me?"

Jason nodded. That was exactly what he wanted to get across today.

Lancaster stood up. He gave Buster a quick pat on the head before Buster slipped back into his tank. Lancaster glanced at his watch, then he grabbed a white lab coat from a hook on the wall.

"It's almost showtime," he said. "Your mother and Maya are waiting for us. You ready?"

"Ready as I'll ever be." Jason stood from his chair. He smoothed his lab coat.

Lancaster opened the door. When they stepped into the hall, a Recode Global employee whizzed by on a scooter. The office hummed with typical weekday morning activities from other employees at work who were typing away at consoles, working on gadgets in labs, or conversating by the water cooler.

They came to another door. Lancaster did a retinal scan and it slid open.

Jason took in a deep breath before he entered a dark space that led to a scaffold. The scaffold was super-high from the ground, but they'd rehearsed it plenty of times, so it wasn't as scary as it used to be.

His mother was reviewing logistics on a tablet while a technician was fitting Maya into her safety harness.

Dr. Pascal smiled at the sight of Jason and Lancaster and came over. "Agent Lancaster," she said, "we're almost ready."

"Please, Dr. Pascal, It's Officer Lancaster now. My agent days are over." The badge on Lancaster's coat gleamed. It read *Recode Global: Chief Security Officer.*

"Right," Dr. Pascal said. "Sorry, force of habit."

"Everything is secured," Lancaster said. "I've got some of my officers planted in the area, and everyone present has been given a serious background check. Also, there will be no catering whatsoever here or in the vicinity."

"That's great to hear." Dr. Pascal said, then she gripped Jason by both shoulders. "You know you're making me beyond proud, right?"

Jason waved his mother way as he glanced at Maya. "*Mom*, do you have to embarrass me now?"

Dr. Pascal looked over at Maya who was still busy with the technician. "Sorry, um . . . knock 'em dead, son!"

"Good luck, kid," Lancaster said. "Try not to screw up this mission, you got me?"

Jason nodded, and Lancaster and his mom left.

Maya made her way over to Jason. She was all set to go on, wearing her safety gear and a tiny wireless headset mic. It looked like someone had done her hair, all fancy, piled up on her head like that.

Jason's suddenly felt all weird. He had never seen Maya look so . . . pretty.

"Are you nervous?" Maya said.

"Me?" Jason swallowed. "Nervous? *Nah.*"

A technician came over and strapped him into his own safety harness. "I could do this with my eyes closed, Maya," Jason continued. "Got this down pat. With my hands tied behind my back. No sweat, I rule this school. Don't you worry."

What was he saying?

The technician handed him his headset mic.

Maya gave him a funny look. "Um, great! So we'll do it just like we rehearsed."

"Yup." Jason put on the mic and wiggled an eyebrow at Maya. "Is my middle name *I've-got-this?*" Ugh. *Too much?*

The technician patted Jason on the shoulder. "You're all set. Good luck." He stepped away, leaving Jason with Maya alone.

Maya tilted her head. "Are you okay?"

Jason straightened. "Yeah, I'm cool as a cucumber." *Cool as a cucumber?!*

"You know," Maya said, "if you like me, you can just tell me that."

Jason's eyes bulged. *Uhhh.*

Maya's face fell, then she turned to take her spot, but just as she did, Jason blurted, "I like you!"

Maya looked back at him. A smile spread across her face. "Great. So do I."

"You do?" Jason said, his heart skipping a beat. *She likes me?*

"I *am* pretty awesome!" Maya said. "So now that that's out of the way, let's focus!"

Jason's heart filled with joy as he took his place beside Maya. *So, she does like me!* He couldn't believe it!

Suddenly, loud music began to play below, and someone from the sound booth let Jason know their mics were live through his earpiece.

Jason's excitement grew, knowing they were about to go on.

"Welcome, everyone!" Ula Varner's voice announced to a crowd below. "It is with great pleasure that I introduce to you Recode Global's first junior interns, Maya Mateo and Jason Pascal!"

Maya and Jason dropped from the scaffold, but instead of free-falling, two ODSCIPs were waiting underneath, just as planned. Maya and Jason's special boots locked onto the ODSCIPs like clockwork. They hovered high above the heads of hundreds of middle school students.

"Hi everybody," Maya said cheerfully as she zoomed around the impossibly white and seamless room. "Are you ready?"

"Yeah!" The crowd whooped.

"I don't think she heard you!" Jason said. "ARE YOU READY?!"

The crowd cheered louder.

Then from the left of the chamber, out came Proto, now equipped to fly. He looked almost like a futuristic dragonfly bot. It was like he'd never been squashed by a crazed corporate warlord, thanks to Dr. Pascal's handiwork. Patty flew out from the right. She looked even cooler than the modified DronePros they had seen at TechToy. They were both followed by a slew of Recode Global drones that looked just like Patty.

"Let me hear you say, *Yeah!*" Proto said over the speakers.

The drones spelled out the word just as the crowd yelled it. The drones lit up in every color of the rainbow as the music hit new heights.

The crowd went wild.

How do you like us now? Proto said in Jason's ear.

Jason gave Proto and Patty a thumbs up.

"We are about to tell you a story," Maya said, "a story about kids just like you and me, some of our greatest advancements on Earth, and a formula for the prosperity of humanity on our planet and beyond!"

As Maya spoke, the drones sky-spelled *AI + HI = The Future Today.*

Jason zoomed by to take his next spot next to Maya at the front. He caught sight of his mom and dad, standing to the side. They had never looked prouder. But he knew what he was about to say next would send Dr. Pascal over the moon.

"What you are about to learn," Jason said, "is that this is story of our present and our future."

Proto and Patty hovered beside Jason and Maya. The music swelled.

Jason looked at Maya and smiled. He felt like he was floating on air, and he *was*. Maya smiled back.

"It is a story," Jason continued, "that is yours to write."

THE END

OR IS IT?

Madame X retreated to her estate on the hillside overlooking the town of Buttonwood, mere miles from Dr. Pascal's suburban home. It had been another long day at the office. She slipped out her Catwoman-like outfit in exchange for a comfortable tracksuit instead. She touched a display on the wall in her living room, and the shades automatically slid down. Her sleek modern couch rotated into the floor and a command center took its place. Madame took a seat as dozens of holographic images lit up above it with video footage of Recode Global's buildings. Alongside the video, other holograms displayed lines and lines of code from Recode's security systems.

Madame X smiled.

She watched Dr. Pascal work on another lesson with Proto. This week, they were discussing variables that affected climate change. Last week, it was restoring clean water to third-world countries. Could this get any more boring?

Soon, things would get exciting. So long as there were misdirected people out there like Dr. Pascal, the universe would need someone like Madame X to fix things. And this time Madame X would trust no one to do the important parts but herself. That was where she had gone wrong.

Madame X sighed. She should have known that. She despised herself for not recognizing her own fallible human thoughts. Being human was unbearable. It was such a punishment, such a prison!

No matter, she would learn from past mistakes. She was already working on another plan. It could take longer than the botched Swift-Tuttle-collision operation, but the outcome would be equally rewarding.

Madame X stared at Dr. Pascal and Proto. "Where there is evil," she said aloud, "there is good."

She swiveled in her chair and studied a portrait hanging on the wall of a very distinguished-looking man, Thaddeus Wilshire II. "Right, Daddy?"

Madame X knew *she* was good.

Very, very good.

THANK YOU
FROM THE AUTHOR

Dear Reader,

Thank you for joining me on an adventure of the mind! I hope you enjoyed reading *The Proto Project* as much as I enjoyed writing it. If you'd like me to know how much you loved the book, I happily accept fan mail as an online review. I read every review, and more importantly, your review will help others decide if the book is right for them. Just keep in mind that your review should be typed by a parent or guardian if you are under the age of thirteen. Please let them know how much you want to share your thoughts with me, and I hope they'll help you out.

Also, if you are not already a Code 7 member, be sure to check out my other book *Code 7: Cracking the Code for an Epic Life*. It is also available in a bilingual Spanish-English edition, too, as *Código 7: Descifrando el código para una vida épica*. Enjoy!

Thanks so much in advance,

Bryan R. Johnson

ACKNOWLEDGEMENTS

When my children were young, I invented stories for them at bedtime. In each story, I incorporated familiar things from their lives and bent reality to take them on journeys into unforeseen worlds. They were always the main characters. At the story's climax, I would announce that I'd finish the story the following night. If that generated clamors of protest, I knew I was on the right track.

Bedtime stories evolved into writing my first book *Code 7: Cracking the Code for an Epic Life*. The enthusiasm from fans gave me great satisfaction, and I had to do just one more: *The Proto Project*.

Neither of these books would have happened without my wonderful editor Cynthea Liu. She embraced me as a novice and made writing joyful. Cynthea and her team spared no effort to make the books the best they could be. Thank you.

Bryan R. Johnson

Visit the website to learn
more about the author and the
story behind the stories!

www.candywrapper.co

Sign up for
author updates

Download the
Discussion Guide

Learn more about
classroom orders

Get a sneak preview of
other books written by
Bryan R. Johnson

CPSIA information can be obtained
at www.ICGtesting.com
Printed in the USA
LVHW081520250222
712022LV00004B/152